You were in a state of suspended animation....

a bodiless voice intoned. *Check your watch and you'll see proof.*

Chase drew in a deep breath and looked down at his wrist.

Satisfied?

"I don't get it. Why have I been trapped here for two years?"

You were forgotten. Events could not proceed to the next level until you were summoned.

"Summoned?"

One woman retained your memory and has called you forth. This woman we speak of has never met you. But she is the key to your future.

"So what am I supposed to do to break the curse? Kiss her?"

Think, Quinn. What is the one thing you have avoided your entire misbegotten life?

A bark of laughter broke through Chase's shock. "You gotta be kidding."

Your deepest fear is what you must face.

"Marriage," Chase muttered. The final frontier.

ABOUT THE AUTHOR

With over eight million copies of her books in print worldwide, Barbara Bretton enjoys a warm place in the hearts of romance readers everywhere. After thirty-plus contemporary and historical novels, this bestselling author is listed in *Foremost Women in the Twentieth Century*, and has been honored with numerous writing awards, including *Romantic Times* Reviewer's Choice awards and a Silver Pen Award from *Affaire de Coeur*. Barbara is a two-time nominee for *Romantic Times* Storyteller of the Year. She loves to hear from her readers, who can reach her at: P.O. Box 482, Belle Mead, NJ 08502.

Books by Barbara Bretton

Barbara Bretton

THE INVISIBLE GROOM

Harlequin Books

TORONTO • NEW YORK • LONDON
AMSTERDAM • PARIS • SYDNEY • HAMBURG
STOCKHOLM • ATHENS • TOKYO • MILAN
MADRID • WARSAW • BUDAPEST • AUCKLAND

For Bonnie Tucker, conference coordinator extraordinaire
and all-around terrific person, who invited me to Houston;
and for Linda Hardcastle (and the brilliant Corundum)
whose VIP-guided tour and hospitality made me love
the city as much as she does. I owe you one, guys!

ISBN 0-373-16554-4

THE INVISIBLE GROOM

Copyright © 1994 by Barbara Bretton

There is a land of the living and a land
of the dead and the bridge is love, the only
survival, the only meaning.

—Thornton Wilder

Prologue

It wasn't that Chase Quinn liked trouble more than other men did, it was just that trouble seemed to find him with amazing regularity.

You didn't have to be a rocket scientist to know he was courting disaster when he decided to head out to the Tucker Mine that morning. But Chase had never been able to resist temptation.

And a hundred-year-old curse was pretty tempting.

Only fools enter here, went the legendary curse. *What you most fear is what you must face.*

Whatever that meant.

"Bad luck just thinkin' about the mine," Chase's stage manager had said the other day. "I heard tell a friend of Rafe Johnson poked his head in there last year and came out bald as a baby's butt."

Chase didn't believe in bad luck. As far as he was concerned, luck was what separated the winners from the losers. Losers waited around, praying lightning would strike or their lottery numbers would finally come up. Winners made their own luck.

From the first day he roared into Vegas on his vintage Harley, Chase had commanded attention. He had fast hands, and a faster mouth, and less than six months after he arrived he was headlining the big room of the newest hotel on the Strip. He conjured doves from silk scarves, sawed beautiful women in half and made grown men disappear. For that he pocketed more money each week than his father had made in his entire lifetime.

Not that his old man had ever given a damn. Not even when the good times came along and the old neighborhood looked at Chase like he was the second coming. The only thing Frank Quinn cared about came inside a bottle of Jack Daniel's. Chase had spent the first sixteen years of his life trying to get his father to really see him and the last sixteen pretending it didn't matter that Frank never did.

But that was behind him now. He didn't need his old man's approval—or anyone else's. The only approval he needed was the rush he felt each time he stepped out onto that darkened stage and turned the night into magic. He was on the fast track now, on his way to stardom, and there was nothing and no one who could knock him back down to earth.

Especially not a woman.

He knew all about promises in the dark, promises that lasted until the sun came up and the heat of passion cooled. He understood that. Hell, even his own mother hadn't stayed around to see how he turned out. Peg Quinn had bolted first chance she got, so don't talk to him about love because Chase didn't buy it.

Love didn't last forever. Sometimes it didn't even last through the night and that was okay as long as you understood right up front that a man couldn't promise forever when he didn't even believe in tomorrow.

The only thing you could count on in life was yourself. When opportunity came along, he knew you had to grab it with both hands because life didn't come with second chances.

And that was what had brought him to the Tucker Mine that day. For one hundred years the mine had been locked tighter than a spinster's bedroom door. Last month some hotshot corporate types had bought up the mine and the surrounding property and were planning to build a theme park. Unfortunately for them, they hadn't banked on the power of an old curse.

"Damn crazy city folk," Chase's assistant had muttered when she heard. "Why don't they stick their noses out of it?"

Henry Henneman, CEO of the corporation, had called for a press conference at ten that morning.

Rumor had it Henneman was going to take the press into the mine to prove, once and for all, that there was no curse associated with it.

"Great idea," Chase said as he gunned the engine of his black Harley. Only thing was, he intended to beat Henneman to it.

ON THE OTHER SIDE of town, Jenna Grey woke with a start. She sat straight up in bed, heart pounding, and told herself it was only a dream. And a foolish one at that. Why, she'd never given the abandoned mine outside of town so much as a second thought.

She leaned back against the headboard and drew in a deep breath, trying to banish the disturbing images from her brain. Dark, winding tunnels . . . a cold rush of wind . . . the sense that nothing would ever be the same again—

"Oh, for heaven's sake!" The tension drained from her body, and she laughed out loud. The symbolism was so obvious, she was surprised it didn't bite her in the ankle. Prenuptial jitters, that's all it was. Just your everyday, run-of-the-mill, wedding morning crazies.

Are you sure it isn't something more? That annoying voice that had been plaguing her for the last two weeks grew louder inside her head. *Are you sure you want to marry Mitch or is it just that you want to rescue him?*

She groaned and lay back against the pillows. There was something terrifying about life-altering questions at seven in the morning on the day of your wedding. Some people rescued stray dogs and cats. Jenna rescued people. Age didn't matter; neither did the sex. If there was a lost or tortured soul within a hundred-mile radius, Jenna's radar went on red alert, and she didn't rest until she found him...or her.

Backstage at the hotel she was known teasingly as St. Jenna, the show girl with a heart of pure platinum, as famous for her generosity as for her beauty. She nursed young girls through failed love affairs, consoled single mothers overwhelmed by responsibility, and to her everlasting dismay, believed she could rescue doomed men.

Ah, yes. Doomed men. She'd read every self-help book on the market, from *Women Who Love Too Much* to *When Good Women Love Bad Men* to *He'll Change...I Know He Will.* But somehow the message never quite made it from her head to her heart.

She'd met Mitch Devane at a party, and while it hadn't been a case of love at first sight, there had certainly been a connection. Mitch was rebounding from a bad marriage. He was lost, vulnerable, needy...everything Jenna loved in a man.

And apparently she was exactly what he wanted in a woman.

Not that he'd ever told her he loved her, but the diamond ring on her left hand surely was proof of that.

Wasn't it?

You know Mitch doesn't love you, Jenna, that annoying voice continued. *Not the way you want him to love you.*

Oh, he loved the way she looked and the way she sounded and the way other men stared at them each time they entered a room. But that deep-down, forever kind of love had somehow eluded them, and she wondered if he knew it, too.

She glanced across the room at his photograph in the silver frame on her dresser. Mitch was a handsome man. Some women might even call him a hunk. Why, then, didn't she feel the slightest surge of sexual chemistry when she looked at him? The question didn't bear close examination. She liked Mitch. She respected him. He needed her.

Marriages had been built on less.

Mitch had said she brought stability to his high-profile life, that she made him feel on top of the world.

Isn't that what Joe said? And Bernard?

"Oh, shut up!" she muttered. So she'd made a few mistakes along the way.

Mistakes? Is that what you call them? Those two rats married other women and asked you to their weddings.

"I'm not going to think about that," she said out loud. "What are the odds of it happening again?"

What were the odds of it happening at all?

She and Mitch might not be the love match of the century, but they were good for each other. She understood how to fit in with his friends and colleagues. She could be an asset for him as a wife.

And Mitch could make her dearest wish come true.

She'd have a husband, a home, a family, everything she'd ever dreamed about growing up on the wrong side of the tracks in Chicago.

And maybe she'd even be happy.

DAMN IT, Chase thought, glancing at his watch. It was almost noon and Henneman still hadn't opened the mine.

He let his glance drift across the faces of the reporters gathered around Henneman. He saw boredom, he saw impatience. He also saw a few curious looks aimed in his direction. Only one of the reporters knew what he was up to and that was because Chase had promised Bob Paxton an exclusive if he'd give him a hand.

A knot of anticipation tightened in his gut and he tried to focus his attention on Henneman, who was now relaying the story of the Tucker curse.

Actually it wasn't a bad story, all things considered. Two men, one woman, the kind of triangle that led to broken hearts no matter what the century. A lonely rancher's wife had been meeting secretly with a handsome gunslinger in the abandoned mine. A wealthy woman, she'd bring a jewel with her each time they met and hide it away against the day she and her lover would leave Nevada behind. Her husband got wind of it and set off toward the mine one night with murder in his heart and too damn much whiskey in his gut. The gunslinger wanted her to run away with him, while the rancher expected her to honor her marriage vows. Desperate to escape the feuding men, the woman plunged deeper into the blackness of the mine.

"The rancher fired a shot at the gunslinger," Henneman said. "The walls of the mine began to shake and they knew they didn't have much time. It doesn't say much for American manhood, but the bodies of those two craven cowards were found just the other side of the entrance and they were facing daylight." Henneman paused for effect. "Some say the wife escaped through a secret exit with the treasure chest of gems, but others say she was the first victim of the curse." His lips drew back in an approximation of a smile. "If you ask me, gentlemen, she just had the misfortune to love two weak men. The mine had nothing to do with that."

"Good story, Henneman," piped up a photographer, "but three men in the last hundred years have tried to reopen the mine, and none of 'em were heard from again."

"Pretty powerful stuff," Bob Paxton commented with a glance toward Chase. "And you think you're going to get Mr. and Mrs. Middle America to pay ten bucks a pop to tempt fate?"

"I don't believe in curses, gentlemen, which brings me to why I've gathered you all here today. The experts I've talked to all believe there's a fortune in jewels hidden away in the mine, and I'm going to give plain folk the chance to find it when the Henneman Western Theme Park opens up. But I need your help. I propose we open the mine right now and we get this nonsense about a curse behind us."

"Forget it," said a gray-haired reporter with a cigarette clamped between his lips. "I'm coming up on retirement. Twenty-four hours a day with my wife is curse enough for me."

"Yeah," said another. "With my luck the damn mine'll cave in, and me just three weeks away from vacation."

Chase glanced around at the reporters with their microcassette recorders held before them like electronic nosegays. It was now or never. He stepped forward. "I have a proposition for you, Henneman."

Instantly Chase was the cynosure of all eyes, just the way he liked it.

Henneman loosed a disgruntled sigh. "If you're one of those environmentalists, you have my word the Henneman Western Theme Park will blend right in with nature. You'll never even know it was here."

Pencil-pushing fool didn't even know who Chase was. "It won't be if you can't convince people the curse doesn't exist."

"That's why I'm here, young man. What do you think I've been doing?"

"I think you've been doing a damn lot of talking but it doesn't seem to me that anyone's been listening."

"And you think they'll listen to you?"

Chase reached deep into the cardboard box at his feet and withdrew a straitjacket, ten yards of heavy metal chain, and a blindfold. "After this they will."

"SO WHAT'S WRONG with this picture?" Jenna muttered as she paced the small waiting room of the Chapel of Wedded Bliss. She tried to ignore the buzz of anxiety inside her head that was growing louder by the minute.

"Now, now, honey." Mavis Sumner, owner of the chapel and a dear friend, patted her on the arm. "Most men come kickin' and screamin' to the altar. He'll show up."

"No, he won't." Her laugh held a hint of hysteria. "They never show up, do they, Mavis? Not once."

"Think positive," Mavis said. "Hold a good thought."

"What time is it?"

"Almost quarter after three."

"I'm going to kill him."

"My first hubby was an hour late, but of course that was because he'd been run over by a streetcar at the corner of Market Street and Main in Flint City. I'm sure as shootin' that isn't the case with you."

"Why don't you just say it and get it over with?" Jenna demanded of her friend. "I picked another loser. Go ahead, Mavis. I can take it."

"There's someone for everyone," Mavis said. "You just haven't got around to the right someone."

"I know Mitch is the one for me." Jenna picked petals from her bouquet as she paced the small room. "He wants a family, same as I do. He knows he can trust me."

"What about love?" Mavis asked gently. "All these weeks and I've never once heard you say you love him." Mavis had been the den mother to scores of Las Vegas show girls since the days of Bugsy Siegel, but she and Jenna had formed an even closer bond. Mavis was the mother Jenna had lost, the grandmother she'd never known, the dear friend she'd always needed. Unfortunately, Mavis was also a pain in the neck.

"I . . . care a great deal for Mitch."

"Ain't the same thing, honey, and we both know it. Somewhere there's a man who can turn your heart inside out. Don't you go settlin' for less while there's breath in your body."

"Mitch needs me," Jenna said. "He loves me."

"He said so?"

"Not in so many words, but he's marrying me, isn't he? That says it all."

"Lots of people get married," Mavis observed, "but damn few of 'em stay that way. You want the truth, honey? I don't think he's showin' up."

"He's showing up."

"I know the signs."

"Mavis, there are no signs. He's just late. Case closed."

Four o'clock came and went.

Then four-thirty.

By five, neither woman could pretend there was going to be a wedding.

"Louse," Jenna muttered as she tossed her bouquet of yellow freesia into a wastebasket. "Stinking rotten beast."

"Good riddance," said Mavis, peering at Jenna over her counted cross-stitch. "Never did think he was the right one for you."

"Now don't go starting that nonsense again."

"Ain't nonsense," Mavis said. "Some women know how to cook. I know who belongs together, and if you ask me it's you and that magician."

"Chase Quinn?" Jenna made a face. "Too slick for his own good." *But those eyes... those sad, lonely eyes...* "I'm going to call Mitch and read him the riot act. He's probably stuck in some ridiculous board meeting."

Mavis led Jenna into the office adjacent to the chapel. A radio leaked easy listening music from a shelf near the window. The older woman motioned toward the telephone on the beige metal desk. "See if he has an explanation, then we'll talk."

"Death is the only explanation I'll accept."

"That's the spirit, honey. There's hope for you yet."

Jenna dialed the telephone, punching in the digits as if each number was her intended's aristocratic nose.

"Good afternoon," trilled the receptionist. "How may I direct your call?"

"Mr. Devane, please."

A pause, then, "May I ask who's calling?"

"The future Mrs. Devane."

A slight clearing of the throat. "I'm sorry, but Mr. Devane has been called out of the country on business."

"In a pig's eye!" Jenna slammed down the phone. "The coward didn't have the guts to jilt me to my face." *Three for three, Jenna. When are you going to learn?*

The soggy radio music stopped abruptly and was replaced by the bland, upbeat voice of the announcer. "Breaking news out at the old Tucker Mine. Illusionist Chase Quinn has pulled the biggest disappearing act of his career. Eyewitnesses who were there for Henry Henneman's press conference said that—"

She and Mavis looked at each other and a simultaneous shiver rose up from the soles of their feet.

"He's gone," Mavis said with a mournful sigh.

"Maybe it's a publicity stunt."

Mavis shook her head. "He's gone," she repeated, "and you were too late to save him."

"Mavis! I didn't even know him. How on earth could I have saved him?"

"Bad business," Mavis said, switching off the radio. "People just don't take curses seriously these days. I should have seen to it that you two found each other, instead of watchin' you wasting your time with men who ain't fit to kiss your hem."

"I don't—" She bit back the words. What difference did it make if some magician disappeared? She had a disappearing act of her own to contend with. The Case of the Vanishing Fiancé.

"Better now than later," Mavis was saying as she patted Jenna's hand. "It's easier to mend a broken heart than a broken marriage any day. He just wasn't the man for you, plain and simple, and I know the one who was."

"This is one for the record books, Mavis. What other woman can say she lost two men in one day?" She twisted off her engagement ring and flung it across the room and then she laughed until she cried.

THE ESCAPE took Chase longer than he'd expected it to, and by the time he stepped out into the sunshine, Henneman and the reporters were climbing into their cars to drive into town.

He stormed toward Henneman's Rolls-Royce. "I risk my butt to prove there's no curse on that damned mine and you guys walk out on me. What gives?"

They ignored him.

Hell, they not only ignored him, they looked right through him like he wasn't even there.

Bob Paxton was standing by Chase's Harley, smoking a cigarette.

"Tell me I'm going to get a front page story out of this," Chase said. "You're not going back on the deal, are you?"

Paxton tossed the cigarette on the ground and stubbed it out with the toe of his boot.

The hairs on the back of Chase's neck rose.

"This is some kind of joke, right, Paxton? I had a little trouble with the straitjacket and this is your way of cutting me down to size."

No reaction.

Not a smile, a groan or a friendly jab in the ribs. Nothing.

Chase reached for the lapels of the reporter's jacket when a giant hand seemed to grab him and hold him fast.

Your friends can't hear you, Chase.

The voice was loud and clear and it reverberated inside his chest. For a moment he wondered if he'd spoken the words but knew he hadn't. Still, they seemed to be making themselves known from a place deep within himself. A place he hadn't known existed.

A place he wasn't sure he wanted to know any more about.

He drew in a deep breath. "I like a joke as much as the next guy, but enough's enough."

Haven't you figured it out yet? Your friends can't see or hear or touch you.

"Gimme a break," Chase snapped over the thudding of his heart. "I don't know what the deal is, but—"

The roar enveloped him, devoured him, made him want to confess to sins he'd never even thought of committing.

Only fools enter here, the unearthly voice intoned as Chase felt himself propelled deep into the heart of the mine, pulled along on a beam of bright white light. *What you most fear is what you must face.*

"Nothing scares me," Chase yelled above the roar. "Not one damned—"

You have been granted two years. Use them well.

With that the light flared for a second then everything went black.

Much later

IT'S TIME.

Chase muttered something and dug deeper into sleep. Six of the Dallas Cowboy cheerleaders were about to explain how to use a tambourine and a water bed to their best advantage, and he didn't want to miss a beat.

Quinn!

The roar inside his chest lifted him onto his feet. Groggy, he glanced around, trying to place his surroundings. "Where are you?"

Everywhere.

It took a second but the whole ridiculous thing came rolling back at him. The mine. The curse. The bright light that had propelled him back into the darkness.

He muttered an oath. "I'm dead," he said, listening to his words echoing in the deserted mine.

Not exactly.

"Not exactly?" He knew life was only an illusion but this was pushing it, even for Quinn. "What the hell does that mean?"

You're a man in transition.

"Uh-huh," said Chase. "Let's try it again. A, I'm alive, B, I'm dead. Pick one."

Such a linear view on such a complex subject. I despair for your future.

"If I have a future I must still be alive."

That is an assumption I would not make.

"Damn it! I don't know what the game is here but if you think I'm going to spend another hour in this godforsaken mine, you're crazy. I have a show tonight. Tell me what I have to do and I'll do it."

You do not have a show tonight, Quinn.

"The hell I don't."

You have not had a show for almost two years.

His heart slammed against the wall of his chest. "Bull."

This is 1994.

"If this is your idea of a joke, it's—"

I am not in the habit of making jokes.

"Why doesn't that surprise me?" Chase muttered, against the rising tide of fear. He was standing there having a conversation with a bodiless voice that seemed to emanate from somewhere inside his chest. If he could accept that, why couldn't he accept the fact that two years of his life had vanished without leaving one single memory behind?

He ran a hand along his cheek and a grin spread across his face. "You had me going, pal, but I've got you dead to rights. No way is this a two-year growth."

Not in the world you knew.

"Not in any world. This is a day's worth of stubble."

You wish a technical explanation?

"Damn straight."

You were in a state of suspended animation.

"Sure I was."

Your bodily functions were slowed to a state able to sustain life and nothing more.

"Right," he said with an admirable display of bravado. "And why don't you beam me aboard while you're at it?"

Check your watch.

"No."

It will prove my point.

"It won't prove jack. Dates can be changed."

But the pull was irresistible. People had laughed when he bought himself the specially made chronograph that did everything but flash his blood pressure reading and bank balance. He drew in a deep breath and glanced at his wrist.

Satisfied?

He leaned against the cold wall of rock. Impossible. No way it could be true. "My contract with the hotel—" His voice caught and he cleared his throat to cover it. "Why not five days or half a century? What's so damn special about two years?"

These things develop in their own time.

"What things?"

Matters of consequence.

"I don't get it. That doesn't explain why I've been trapped here for two years."

You were forgotten. It was as if you had never existed. Events could not proceed to the next level until you were summoned.

"Summoned?"

One woman retained your memory and has called you forth.

It made him sound like a trained lapdog, but he was in no position to argue semantics. Still his curiosity was piqued. "Gotta be someone I dated." It was nice to know one of his old girlfriends still carried a torch.

Your former flames have found new loves. The woman we speak of has never met you.

"So how is she summoning me?"

You will soon find out. She is the key to your future.

"She knows I'm coming?"

She knows nothing at all.

"What am I supposed to do? Kiss her? Paint her house? Buy her a lottery ticket?"

Think, Quinn. What is the one thing you have avoided your entire misbegotten life?

A bark of laughter broke through Chase's shock. "You gotta be kidding."

Your deepest fear is what you must face if you are to pick up the threads of your life.

"Marriage," Chase muttered.

The final frontier.

Chapter One

Two weeks later—Tuesday night

Jenna raised her champagne glass high and toasted the naked man on the pedestal.

"Ladies," she announced with great ceremony, "I give you the perfect man. He can't talk, he can't think, he can't use the remote control. It doesn't get any better than this."

"He should be taller," said Liz, the receptionist at Fantasy Weddings of Las Vegas, The Place Where Dreams Come True.

"More chest hair," said Grace, the bookkeeper. "I like them hairy."

Rosalia Suarez, one of the young artisans on staff, gave him a quick look and shrugged her shoulders. "Great pecs, but don't you think it's time you found one who can breathe, Jenna?"

"Forget it." Jenna stared up at her creation. "Once they start breathing they're nothing but trouble."

She should know. One year, eleven months and twenty-seven days ago she'd been left standing at the altar when Mitch Devane ran off to Geneva with his secretary. His *homely* secretary.

Liz made a show of circling the naked Adonis. "There's something awfully...familiar about him," she said, grinning at the raucous catcalls from the other women. "I mean it." She turned toward Jenna, who was pouring herself some more champagne. "Why is it I feel like I've met this guy?"

"In your dreams, girlfriend," Grace piped up. "If men like this actually existed, women wouldn't need chocolate."

Jenna held her breath as her friend continued circling the statue like a small, blond bloodhound.

Liz stopped and inspected the rear view. "Impressive."

"Thank you," said Jenna, downing more champagne. "I worked hard on those." Leave it to Liz to take the low road. There was no denying his buns were impressive, but for Jenna it was his hands that had captured her imagination. Big hands. Powerful hands. Magic hands.

"That's him!"

Golden droplets of champagne splashed across the front of Jenna's T-shirt.

"Who?"

"That magician. Oh, you know, the one who disappeared three years ago."

"Two years ago," Jenna corrected automatically, then wished she'd kept her mouth shut when she saw the avid light in Liz's blue eyes.

"What was his name? Chase. Chase Quinn."

Jenna brushed at the champagne on her shirt then licked her fingertips. She wasn't the kind of woman who wasted good champagne. "Is there a likeness?"

"A likeness?" Liz's gaze drifted down his torso. "Honey, this is his double." She looked over at Jenna. "Firsthand knowledge or a good imagination?"

You could hear a pin drop in the normally noisy studio.

"Imagination," she said dryly. "And newspaper clippings."

"This one's going to put us all on the map," Rosalia piped up as she poured more wine into her paper cup. "When they see what you've done with Fantasy Man, business will go through the roof."

"Let's just hope we make it through the first year," Jenna said, smiling at her young protégé. "I owe Mavis that much, at least." When Mavis Sumner decided to retire from the wedding chapel business, she'd offered Jenna the first opportunity to buy her out, and Jenna, weary of working as a show girl, had leapt at the chance. Anything that brought her closer to her goal.

"We'll be a smash," said Rosalia with the assurance of the young and unjaded. "Las Vegas is the wedding capital of the world, and Fantasy Weddings is the best place in town."

"From your mouth to God's ear," Liz murmured, still eyeing the statue with great curiosity. "Marriage isn't what it used to be. People used to believe it lasted forever. Now they get married the way we used to change slipcovers."

"Good," Jenna snapped. "And every time they do get married, I hope they come here so we can make a fortune."

"Aren't we sounding cynical," Liz observed.

"I'm a realist. You don't have to believe in hearts and flowers to make this business work. All I want is a nice big fat bottom line and I'll be happy."

There it was again, that silence she'd noticed before.

"Why are you looking at me like that?" she demanded. "I'm just telling the truth." Fantasy Weddings was a means to an end for Jenna, the quickest route to the nest egg that would enable her to one day have time to devote to her sculpting. She offered a lopsided, champagne grin. "Besides, it beats being a show girl hands down."

Grace sighed and drained her paper cup. "I don't know about the rest of you, but it's time I headed for home. Tomorrow's going to be a zoo. We have twenty-two weddings scheduled and who knows how many walk-ins."

Liz turned to Rosalia. "Need a lift into town?"

Rosalia shook her head. "Gil is waiting outside."

Jenna shot a quick look at the young girl. "I thought the two of you had broken up."

Rosalia's full cheeks reddened. "That was just a—a misunderstanding. He said he was sorry."

Jenna's eyebrows lifted as she struggled to rein in her temper. "Sorry? The man hit you, Rosalia. Sorry doesn't quite cut it."

Rosalia placed a hand on Jenna's forearm. "He's a good man, Jenna. Really he is. All he needs is someone to love him."

"What about you?" Jenna persisted. "Don't you need someone to love—"

"Rosa." Gil stood in the doorway. He was short, but he made up in muscle mass what he lacked in height, and his talent for intimidation only added to the illusion of substance. "Get moving."

Jenna was not in the mood for intimidation. "Why don't you join us, Gil?" she said in an even tone. "We're celebrating."

He ignored Jenna as if she weren't there. "I work tomorrow morning," he said. "You're keeping me up."

"I'll bring Rosalia home," Jenna said, still controlling her tone. "You don't have to worry about her."

Gil turned slowly toward her, and Jenna felt the hairs on the back of her neck rise in response. *Bastard,* she thought, maintaining her pleasant smile. *If I had my way, you'd be behind bars for what you've done to Rosalia.*

"You're not keeping her here for any reason, are you?" he asked Jenna.

"Absolutely not. This is a party. Rosalia's free to go whenever *she* chooses."

His eyes narrowed and Jenna knew her words had found their mark. *Good,* she thought. *Not everyone is afraid of you.*

"I'm ready to go, Gil," Rosalia said, a nervous smile fluttering at the corners of her mouth. "I know you have to get up real early tomorrow morning."

You don't have to apologize to him, Jenna thought.

She turned toward Rosalia and lowered her voice. "We're going to talk," she said, trying to ignore the pleading look in the young woman's chocolate brown eyes. She knew all about the urge to rescue men and how it could backfire, and in Rosalia's case she was risking much more than a broken heart. "You deserve better than this."

"Rosa." Gil's voice held more than a hint of anger.

Rosalia quickly grabbed her purse and sweater from the back of a chair then left with him.

"He has her well-trained," Liz remarked.

"I wouldn't push him, Jenna," Grace said as she gathered up her own belongings. "The way he looked at you—" She shook her head in dismay. "I think he wanted to hit you."

"Let him try it," Jenna said. "I'll have him in jail so fast his beady little eyes'll spin."

"Don't bet on it," Liz said. "My Frank says the wrong person always ends up hurt in these cases."

"I worry about her," Grace said. "I wish she'd just meet some nice boy and settle down."

"Same here," said Jenna, starting for the door. "Maybe I should go out there and—" She tripped and caught herself by grabbing for the back of a gilt and velvet chair.

"See?" Liz sounded smug. "I told you you've had too much champagne. You can't even walk."

"I tripped," she said. "That has nothing to do with champagne."

Liz glanced at the ground. "Tripped over what?"

Jenna followed her friend's gaze and saw nothing but shiny marble floor. A weird sensation nipped at the back of her neck, almost as if someone was watching her. But there was no one there besides her plaster of paris creation and her two employees. "There was something there," she said, pointing toward her feet. "I know there was."

"Uh-huh," said Liz, meeting Grace's eyes.

"You don't believe me."

"That's right," said Grace. "We don't believe you."

"Go home, you two," she said. "I'll be fine." She looked at the spot where she'd tripped, still saw nothing, then made to catch up with Rosalia.

Liz blocked her way. "It didn't work with Sarah. It isn't going to work with Rosalia." Sarah had actually married the louse in question and ended up in both the hospital and divorce court.

"But maybe if I—"

"You can't save the world, Jenna. She'll find her own way."

"That guy is dangerous," Grace chimed in. "Don't tangle with him over Rosalia. I'm afraid he might hurt you."

Jenna made a muscle. "He'd lose," she said, trying to lighten the suddenly dark atmosphere.

Liz mustered up a slight smile then pulled her car keys from the pocket of her slacks. "Get your stuff," she commanded Jenna. "You've had too much champagne to drive."

Jenna took another deep swallow. "I haven't had nearly enough champagne," she said with a loopy grin.

"You don't really think I'm going to let you drive yourself home in that condition, do you? Not with opening day tomorrow."

Jenna plucked her own car keys from the table-top then tossed them to her friend. "There. Does that make you feel better? I won't drive."

"Now I can rest easy," said Grace. "See you two tomorrow."

"Get your stuff," Liz repeated as the door swung shut after Grace. "It's time to call it a night."

Jenna glanced at her watch. "It's not even midnight."

"I don't know about you," Liz said, "but I turn into a pumpkin when the clock strikes twelve."

"I'd pay to see that."

"Let's go."

Jenna shook her head. "I still have some work to do."

"How will you get home?"

"I won't. I'll sleep here."

Liz wrapped her arms about her middle and shivered. "This place is too spooky for me. I'd never be able to sleep. Especially not with Adonis staring down at me."

"Then go home," Jenna urged, pushing her friend toward the door. "I'll turn on the alarm system. I'll be fine."

"You'll call me if you need help?"

"Absolutely." She grinned. "And won't Frank just love me for that?"

Liz relaxed and cast a last, longing look at the life-size statue in the middle of the room. "Life is cruel," she said with a shake of her head. "It's hard to believe my Frank and Wonder Boy are even the same species."

"Frank loves you," Jenna said softly as the harsh light of reality penetrated her champagne fog. "That makes all the difference."

"I suppose," said Liz, not sounding terribly convinced. "But what I'd give for just one night with a god."

What about when the man in question looks like a fallen angel? Jenna thought as she locked up after Liz, then set the alarm.

Now there was a dangerous question. She poured herself some more champagne and considered her creation. "You're allowed to look like a fallen angel," she said to the statue. "You're not real." She couldn't save him or reform him or fall in love with him, which made him just about the perfect man in her book.

Two years ago, on the day she'd been left standing at the altar, magician Chase Quinn had vanished inside the abandoned Tucker Mine on the outskirts of town, never to be heard from again. At first they'd called it the publicity act of the century, the greatest stunt since Houdini and the locked safe. But as the days went by, then the weeks, people began to wonder if maybe—just maybe—there was something to all that talk about curses.

Henry Henneman put aside his plans to turn the mine into a theme park. The Paradise Hotel found a new and less charismatic magician to take Quinn's place, and if the new guy wasn't as big a box office draw, at least he was reliable, which was something Chase Quinn had never been.

After a few months no one remembered his name.

Except Jenna.

She couldn't say how it started. Maybe it was the coincidence of his disappearance and her non-wedding happening on the same day. She didn't want to think it could be anything more than that. She'd seen the flutter of anticipation his proximity had created in even the most jaded of show girls, and she'd determined right from the beginning to stay as far away from trouble as she possibly could.

And he would be trouble. Men who looked the way he looked couldn't be anything but trouble for a woman like Jenna. A bad boy with magic hands and a look of sorrow in his eyes that pierced her through to her soul. Even though she had a weakness for men in need of redemption, something inside her had warned that Chase Quinn would be her undoing.

So she'd stayed out of his way, spending her free time between shows tucked safely away in the dressing room, plotting the day when she'd have enough money to say goodbye to being a part-time show girl and hello to being a full-time artist.

She tilted her head and studied the statue, admiring both his form and her ability to bring it to life. A safe, manageable fantasy...as safe and manageable as the life she'd created for herself.

Safe and manageable and lonely.

She stumbled over to the sideboard where the champagne bottle rested in a paint bucket of ice cubes. "Damn you, Chase Quinn," she muttered as she poured the rest of the liquid into her glass. "Why can't I stop thinking about you?"

She hadn't planned on recreating his likeness, muscle by muscle, sinew by sinew. The original idea had been to duplicate Michelangelo's *David* and give him a twentieth-century twist. But, fool that she was, she'd decided to improve upon a masterpiece by pumping up the biceps, sculpting the chest, roughing up those classical features, until she'd found herself standing face to face with a man she'd never meet.

For the past few days she'd had the oddest feeling each time she looked at the statue, almost as if she expected it to spring to life the way Ava Gardner had in that old movie, *One Touch of Venus*. One morning last week she'd opened up the workroom behind the chapel and caught the scent of woodsmoke and spice in the air, but it vanished before she could identify its source. Then yesterday she'd found the cushions on her sofa scrunched up as if someone had been sleeping on them, and of course that was ridiculous. She was the only one crazy enough to sleep there with all those dead-eyed statues to keep her company.

Huge drops of rain pinged against the windows, a cold, gloomy kind of rain that suited her mood, and through it she heard the distant rumble of thunder.

"To you, Chase Quinn." She raised her glass in the direction of the statue. "Wherever you are, I'm glad you're not here."

There was something too sad about the look in his eyes, something too dark and compelling for her ever to feel anything but glad that he was only a statue and not a part of her life. She knew the type, all dark and brooding and filled with angst-ridden secrets, the kind of man who could turn a woman's heart inside out without even trying. Where were the uncomplicated men America was famous for, big strong healthy guys who sprang fully formed from perfect sitcom families, guys whose only worry was whether their favorite football team would make it to the Super Bowl?

They were out there, she knew they were, but they might as well be invisible, for their presence never registered on Jenna. No, life would be too easy if she fell in love with an uncomplicated, loving man. A man like that might even make her happy.

Lightning crackled outside, and she turned to the window in time to see the night sky flash a brilliant, electric white.

Maybe you should have gone home with Liz. The thought of spending the night alone in the empty building suddenly sounded less appealing than it had a few moments ago, and she raised her glass to her lips to dull the sharp edges of apprehension.

"Don't you think you've had enough of that stuff?"

She shook her head, trying to clear the cobwebs. Her conscience was sounding particularly loud tonight.

"Four glasses, Jenna. You don't look like the kind who can hold her booze."

She might be hearing voices, but at least she was hearing *great* voices. Deep, sensuous, stirring. The way he said her name was enough to make her knees buckle. A low, erotic rumble that could be a lesser woman's undoing. If she was going crazy, at least she was doing it with style. It took a woman with a splendid imagination to conjure up a teetotaling conscience with high-voltage sex appeal.

"You brought me here," the voice commanded. "Aren't you going to turn around?"

Don't panic, Jenna. You're not crazy, you're just drunk on cheap champagne.

She turned around. The statue smiled down at her. But that wasn't possible, was it? Statues couldn't smile, except maybe at Disney World, and this sure wasn't any place you'd find Minnie and Mickey. She blinked, wishing she felt more clearheaded, because for a minute she swore there were two of them.

"Don't scream," he said. "The acoustics in this place are murder."

Her jaw dropped open. "You can talk!"

His statue brow furrowed. "Why wouldn't I be able to talk?"

"Because you're a statue, that's why." Or had been one the last time she looked. She stared at him, wishing she hadn't been so intent upon finishing all the champagne in the state of Nevada. Statues didn't come to life. Statues stayed on their pedestals where they belonged and they didn't complain about the acoustics.

She watched, amazed, as he flexed a few of his statue muscles to considerable effect.

"Still think I'm a statue?"

"I don't know what I think." She gulped down the rest of her champagne as the answer dawned. "Liz put you up to this, didn't she?" Liz had probably sneaked him in through the back entrance, and now those stinkers were all gathered outside laughing. "This is some kind of stupid practical joke." The kind that turned a woman's hair prematurely gray.

"Which one is Liz?"

"The small blonde with the perverse sense of humor."

He shook his head. "She had nothing to do with it."

"Oh, don't lie to me. This is exactly the kind of rotten thing she'd do. No wonder she made such a big deal about your—" She barely stopped in time.

"She's the one who liked my butt."

"Don't look so smug. Liz has never met a butt she didn't like."

He flexed his gluteus maximus.

"Stop doing that!"

"Do you like my—"

"Say one more word and so help me I'll—" Once again she brought herself up short. "I'm not going to discuss this with you." She might be drunk but she had a few shreds of dignity left. She narrowed her eyes in his general direction. "The joke's over, Adonis. The least you can do is cover yourself. I feel like I'm at a peep show."

"There's nothing here you haven't seen before."

"Maybe not, but it wasn't talking back to me before. You've earned your money. Now get down from that pedestal and show me where you stashed the real statue so I can put him back where he belongs."

It happened so quickly she couldn't believe her eyes. His expression hardened. His smile faded and his mouth settled into the elegant, strong line she'd created with her own fingers from photographs of Quinn. She knew each angle and plane of jaw and cheekbone, each—

"You're a statue," she mumbled. "Of course you're a statue." He'd never been anything *but* a statue. How on earth could she have imagined that a hunk of plaster of paris was a living, breathing man?

Suddenly he winked. "Still think I'm a statue?"

"Yes," she said hotly. "And statues are meant to be seen and not heard."

"Should've thought about that before you conjured me up, Jenna."

"I didn't conjure anything," she snapped. "You're the magician, not me."

"Is something wrong?" he asked, turning slowly. His muscles rippled with each movement. "Do I need some repair work?"

"What you need is a pair of Jockey shorts."

He bent down and reached for the white cloth she'd used to cover the statue earlier from prying eyes. Draping it over his torso toga fashion, he climbed down from his pedestal. "Feel better now?"

Suddenly she realized what was happening. "I don't feel anything at all. I'm asleep. This is all a bad dream." That had to be the explanation. She'd had a million dreams that seemed more vivid than real life, and this was one more to add to the list.

"You've had a hell of a lot of champagne, but sleeping it off isn't going to make a difference." He moved toward her.

"Take another step," she warned, "and I won't be held responsible."

He came closer. She held her ground. It was her dream and she'd be damned if she backed away from the challenge in his eyes.

"You want me," he said. "That's why you made that statue."

She laughed out loud. "You can't possibly know what I want."

He closed the distance between them. She did find it strange that he could be on his pedestal and right there in front of her at the same time, but fantasies didn't play by the rules. "You want me as much as I want you."

He's right . . . you know he's right . . .

He drew her into his arms, and the last of her defenses shattered. For years she'd told herself it didn't matter, that she didn't need, didn't want the madness that came with love and desire. But dear God, how could she have forgotten the way it felt to be so close to a man that his heartbeat became yours, to feel his breath, sweet and hot, against your skin, to know that you would never again draw a breath that wasn't somehow connected with him.

Because this is different... because nothing has ever been like it is now...

Everything about him, everything about the moment, was perfect, if only because none of it was real. Illusions couldn't break your heart, only real life could do that, and this most definitely was not real life. In a little while she'd wake up with a terrible champagne hangover, and this interlude would be nothing more than a fuzzy memory. Why not surrender to the moment?

He cupped her face with his hands, those hands that she knew so well. She'd fallen in love with those hands. The way they looked. The way the simple thought of them had made her feel in the heart of the night when she was alone with nothing but her imagination and a loneliness that cut so deep she thought she'd die of it.

"Beautiful..." His voice was dark as the sky beyond the window. "So beautiful."

She found herself falling more deeply under his spell. She'd often dreamed in living color, but never had her dreams blossomed in the third dimension. How long had it been since she'd felt this sweet rush of heat, seen this glorious burst of light? Years...a lifetime. She had the peculiar sensation that every day, every minute, every second that had come before had only existed to bring her to this moment and to this man.

His hands caressed her shoulders, her upper arms, moved slowly toward the swell of her breasts, and her back arched as she moved closer.

Let this be real, she thought. *Let this—*

His mouth, that hard, proud mouth, slanted across hers, claiming her, body and breath and soul. She placed her hands flat against his magnificent chest and opened her eyes, wanting to drink in the sight of him.

His eyes were open, too. Golden eyes. Somehow she'd known that was how it would be.

The primal drumbeat deep within her body grew louder as he gathered her in his arms. *This is the one you've been waiting for... don't be afraid—*

"No!" She'd had too much champagne, but not enough to do anything this crazy. She pointed toward the pedestal in the middle of the room. "Get back up there *right now*. This dream has gone far enough."

No sooner were the words out of her mouth than he was up on the pedestal where he belonged.

"Is this what you want?" he asked, looking as glorious and godlike as when she had first created him.

"Yes," she said, feeling light-headed and half mad. "I want you to stay there and mind your own business."

"I don't mind humoring you, Jenna, but sooner or later we're going to have to talk about getting married." She rummaged around behind the workbench and found a painter's drop cloth then dragged a stepladder over to the pedestal.

"Give me a break," he protested. "I've been trapped in that damn mine for two years—"

A big-mouth statue with a history? "Oh, shut up! Up until last month you were a bag of plaster of paris." She draped the sheet over his head and let it fall.

Carefully she climbed down the stepladder and settled in a heap on the floor.

Tomorrow, she thought wearily, as she closed her eyes. *It will all make sense tomorrow...*

Chapter Two

Is that the best you can do, Quinn?

Chase climbed down from the pedestal and sat next to the sleeping woman. "Is it my fault she's had too much to drink? She thought I was naked." Maybe it was a good thing she'd mistaken the statue for him. Reality might have been too weird a concept.

Your only hope of redemption and the woman can't keep her eyes open.

He glared at the room in general. "Tell me something I don't know." That was the trouble with disembodied voices of doom. A man didn't know where to aim his dirty looks.

Frankly, I don't think this is going to work.

Jenna Grey murmured something in her sleep then stretched her long, show-girl legs. She was wearing one of those slinky black cat suits that made good bodies great and great bodies an occasion of sin. Jenna Grey ranked as one of the seven deadly.

"It's going to work," he said as much for himself as his doomsaying friend. "She owns a wedding chapel. How much more perfect can it get?"

And the shoemaker goes barefoot.

Chase snorted. "What's that supposed to mean?"

She doesn't believe in you.

"She doesn't have to believe in me. All she has to do is marry me." And fast. He jerked his head in the direction of the statue. "She wouldn't have built that if she didn't feel something for me."

You are an estimable representative of the male specimen in his prime. As an artist she appreciates the symmetry of your form.

"This whole thing would be a hell of a lot easier if I didn't keep disappearing on her."

If she had summoned you earlier, that would be a lesser problem. The closer the deadline approaches, the greater the pull exerted by other forces.

"You're stacking the odds against me."

You stacked the odds yourself by the way you chose to live your life. Are you afraid you cannot attract her to your side?

"Hell, no. She wants me."

She pushed you away.

"Doesn't matter. She still wants me."

That doesn't mean she will consent to become your wife, and you have less than one week remaining to you.

"You're not going to hold me to that deadline, are you?" Chase protested. "Hell, it took almost the entire two years just to get back here."

The rules are the rules. If you find the task too difficult—

"Leave it to me," Chase said. "I've been told I have a way with women." He grimaced as his chest seemed to fill with the entity's laughter. "Damn, but I wish you'd stop that. Why don't you make yourself visible?"

I am visible. You simply haven't learned to see.

Chase leapt to his feet and began pacing the room. "Where do you get this stuff, from a fortune cookie?"

You're ever impetuous, Quinn. You have many more obstacles to overcome.

"Name one."

That is not for me to say. You must find out for yourself. What transpires in the next few days will determine your destiny.

Chase inclined his head in Jenna's direction. Her amazing body was curled around the pedestal of the statue. "She'll marry me."

I would not be so sure of that.

He thought of the way she'd felt in his arms, and a blast of heat radiated outward from his gut. "It's a done deal."

Even your magic might not be enough to make it so.

"I won't need magic."

You will need more magic than even you can imagine. You have until one minute after midnight, Sunday morning to convince a total stranger to become your wife.

Chase blew right by that statement. "So what happens after she marries me? The curse is broken and we can divorce, right?"

Jenna pushed up on one elbow and aimed a bleary-eyed glance at his plaster of paris likeness. "Oh, shut up!" she snapped, stifling a yawn. "I need my sleep." With that she conked out again.

I wish you luck, Chase Quinn.

"What do you mean, you wish me luck? Are you going somewhere?"

From this moment hence you are on your own.

"But wait! What about the curse—how will I know when it's broken?"

You'll know, my friend. You'll know.

Wednesday

ROSALIA SUAREZ ARRIVED at work a few minutes before nine o'clock the next morning. Jenna was seated at her desk, doing her best to pretend she hadn't consumed enough champagne the night before to float a battleship.

The young woman leaned forward and peered into Jenna's eyes. "You look terrible."

"Thank you," Jenna mumbled, wishing once again that the golden wine had never been invented. "And I feel even worse."

Rosalia's soft laugh hammered inside her head.

"Please!" Jenna clamped her hands over her ears. "Have mercy on me."

"It's her first hangover," Liz called from her desk in the main lobby.

"And her last," Jenna stated. "Alcohol should come with a warning label attached."

"All things in moderation," Grace said with a nod of her head.

Moderation, Jenna thought. Now there was a commodity in short supply, if last night's dreams were any indication. She'd always envied women who enjoyed erotic flights of fancy each night as soon as the lights went out, but her dreams usually ran toward less interesting natural phenomena.

But not last night. Maybe it was the champagne or maybe it was the deep, aching loneliness that was her constant companion—she didn't know exactly what it was that had been at the heart of it, but last night she'd found herself suspended somewhere between reality and dreams...and wishing she never had to wake up.

The way he'd touched her as if he knew her body better than she knew it herself. The scent of wood-smoke and spice as he pulled her into his arms. The pooling heat at the top of her thighs.

The knowledge that whatever happened, it had somehow been preordained a long, long time ago and there was nothing she could do to stop it—

A voluptuous shiver rippled upward from the soles of her feet. *A dream,* she told herself. *That's all it was.* She'd awakened this morning to find herself curled around the base of the Quinn statue in a most intimate fashion. Drinking too much was one thing. Acting like a fool was something else, and she thanked God no one had caught her hugging an inanimate object as if it was the answer to her prayers.

But the dream had been so real, so vivid, that for a moment she thought she caught the scent of wood smoke in the air, felt the heat of his kisses against her skin.

"Are you sure you're all right?" Rosalia asked. "You look so sad."

Both Liz and Grace turned toward her, concern evident on their faces.

"I noticed that before," Liz said. "Right after you finished the statue."

"I didn't want to say anything," Grace offered, "but I said to my hubby, 'Jenna's just not happy these days.'"

"That's the problem with this place," Jenna said, touched despite herself. "You're all too darned nosy for your own good."

"We care," Rosalia said, touching Jenna's forearm. "We hate to see you looking so unhappy."

What could she say to that? These people meant the world to her, but not even her friends' concern could fill the aching emptiness that was her heart. Last night, for one brief moment, she'd thought she'd found the answer, but that had been a dream that had as much to do with too much champagne as it had with too many nights spent alone and lonely.

"C'mon, guys," she said, clapping her hands together. "We open for business in less than three hours. Let's get moving!"

She checked the flower arrangements, the music, and made certain the newly repaired air-conditioning system would be up to the day ahead. The statues of Cleopatra, Elvis and Marilyn Monroe were in place in the entry lobby, awaiting the remaining likenesses.

"We'd better give Mike a nudge," she said to Rosalia, "or we'll be dragging those statues over here during the first wedding."

Rosalia grinned. "I've been dying to get my hands on Mr. Wonderful one last time."

Everyone had teased Jenna about her extraordinary concern for the statue of the missing magician. Normally she handled the purely creative aspects of the job, leaving the final execution to her team of artisans. However, she alone had seen Quinn through from pencil sketch to the application of a remarkably lifelike plastic film that made him seem almost human.

Maybe too human.

She forced her thoughts to more pressing concerns.

"How did everything go last night? Was Gil upset that you kept him waiting?"

Two patches of color flamed on Rosalia's cheeks. "He understood when I explained it to him."

Jenna could imagine how well Gil understood the young woman's explanation. More than once Jenna had been on the receiving end of Gil's verbal jabs when Rosalia worked overtime and his dinner wasn't ready. "You shouldn't have to explain it to him, Rosie. That's what I've been trying to tell you."

"I don't want to talk about this, Jenna. You just don't understand."

"Listen to me." Jenna took Rosalia's hand in hers and forced the young woman to meet her eyes.

"I'm here for you. If you ever want to make a change, come to me. I can help."

Rosalia turned away, but not before Jenna noticed a swell of purple just beneath the collar of her cotton blouse. "We'd better help Mike get those statues in place."

We're going to talk about this again, Rosie, Jenna thought as she followed the younger woman out to the studio across the parking lot. At least the men Jenna had tried to save had only broken her heart. Rosalia's Gil had done much more damage than that, and it scared Jenna to think of what the future might hold.

Rosalia pushed open the door to the studio, then held it for Jenna.

"I can't believe you slept here last night," the younger woman said as the door closed behind them. "This place gives me the creeps."

Jenna looked across the room at the last three statues waiting to be brought to the chapel. Helen of Troy. Indiana Jones.

Chase Quinn.

Metaphorically girding her loins, she sidled over toward the likeness of the missing magician.

"Do you see anything...different about this statue?" she asked Rosalia in as casual a tone as she could manage.

"He needs a shave," Rosalia said, then giggled. "I don't know how to break it to you, Jenna, but he's a statue. What can be different?"

Which was exactly what Jenna kept repeating to herself as she supervised the removal of the figures from the studio to the main lobby. Statues didn't climb down from their pedestals and try to seduce the woman who made them. *Remember that, Jenna,* she thought.

Quinn's likeness was the last to be moved.

"Damn," said Mike Locaro, her handyman, gripping the statue by its waist. "I can't budge this guy."

Rosalia grabbed the statue's ankles. "Now try."

Still nothing.

"What'd you do, Ms. Grey, pour lead in his feet?" Mike was red-faced with exertion.

"You wimps!" Jenna took up a position near the statue's shoulders. "Liz and I dragged this fellow across the—" She drew in her breath sharply. "Did you see that?"

Mike and Rosalia exchanged looks. "See what?" asked Rosalia.

"He winked."

"Sure he did, Ms. Grey," said Mike in a kindly tone.

"I thought you finished all the champagne last night," Rosalia said.

"I'm not joking and I'm not drunk. I know what I saw. He winked."

The three of them stared at the statue. The statue stared back.

"He's not moving, Jenna," said Rosalia in a cautious voice.

"Dead as a doornail," Mike observed dryly.

"Don't talk to me like I'm certifiable," Jenna snapped. "I'm not making this up."

"You have to admit this is a little...weird," Rosalia said.

Heat rose to Jenna's cheeks as she stared at the motionless statue. *Get a grip before they call for the men in the white coats.* "Maybe it was the lighting," she conceded. "I didn't sleep well last night. I suppose anything's possible." She didn't necessarily believe it but for the sake of unity it seemed the thing to say. *Maybe you're going crazy, Jenna. Have you thought of that?*

BY MIDNIGHT thirty-six couples had been joined in holy matrimony at Fantasy Weddings. Mavis had planned to attend at least a few of them, but her gentleman friend was feeling under the weather, and she opted to nurse him with chicken soup and lots of T.L.C. Mavis's presence was missed, but Jenna called her that evening to let her know that Fantasy Weddings was just what they'd expected it to be—a smash.

Jenna was both exhausted and elated when she waved goodbye to the evening shift and stepped outside into the cool Las Vegas night. She'd also gone through two boxes of Kleenex. That surprised her. Given her checkered premarital history, who would have thought she'd be so sentimental about weddings?

Or so uneasy.

She couldn't have asked for a better opening day, yet for some reason she'd found herself peering repeatedly over her shoulder, almost as if she expected to find someone peering back at her.

Like right now.

She paused a few yards away from her VW bug and turned to scan the area. Not a soul in sight. Not a sound to be heard. In fact, the only noise she'd heard in the past hour was a car door opening and closing. So why couldn't she shake the certainty that she wasn't alone? It was that strange, haunted feeling that had been bothering her for days without rhyme or apparent reason.

"The champagne," she muttered, opening her car door and climbing inside. The stuff had the half-life of uranium. "I will never drink champagne again as long as I live."

"You'll drink it at our wedding." The voice was sweet and dark as brandy and eerily familiar.

Her heart slammed into her rib cage, and she gripped the steering wheel for support. "I'm stone cold sober. I am not hearing voices."

"I've been waiting out here for two hours. What took you so long?"

A bead of sweat snaked its way down her spine. "I'm overtired. I need to go home and get a good night's sleep." *That's not going to make a difference, Jenna. This is real.*

She tossed her pocketbook onto the passenger seat then stared, wide-eyed, as it came bouncing right back at her.

"Watch where you throw that thing!"

"What on earth—" She scrambled up onto her knees and peered behind her seat. Not that there was any place for someone to hide in a VW bug, but you couldn't be too careful.

"Not back there," the incredibly sexy male voice said. "Over here."

"Over here?" she repeated. "Where's here?"

"Next to you."

"There's nobody next to me." She knew that voice, but from where?

"Look again. The passenger seat."

She took a good hard look. It was dark inside the car, but not so dark that she'd miss the fact that someone was sitting next to her. The seat was empty.

She looked again.

Or was it?

Since when did the passenger seat look so squashed and flat? If she didn't know better, she'd think someone was sitting on it.

"Yeah. Right." She leaned forward to touch the cushion then let out a shriek of dismay as a hand seemed to clamp itself around her wrist and hold her fast.

"Don't yell," the male voice ordered. "I have enough trouble right now as it is. I don't need the cops asking questions you can't answer."

She lashed out with her free hand and heard a resounding crack as it met some very real, very human resistance.

"Damn it, lady! Are you trying to kill me?"

She pulled her hand away, pulse pounding wildly in her ears. "Kill you? I can't even *see* you." *Listen to yourself, Jenna! You're talking to thin air.*

"Hey, that's your problem, not mine."

"I am not going to have this bizarre conversation," she said out loud as she started the engine. "I am going to drive home, climb into bed and sleep this off." Whatever it was.

"We have to talk."

She backed the car out of its parking spot.

"I'm not going away until we talk."

She drove down the drive and onto the street.

"Damn it, lady, I'm running out of time."

She maneuvered around a stalled limousine and past the entrance to the Paradise Hotel, where she and Chase Quinn both had worked.

"My old stomping grounds," said the voice.

One second the passenger seat was empty. The next second Chase Quinn, in all his outlaw glory, was sitting there grinning at her.

She slammed on the brakes, skidding across two lanes of traffic until the VW rolled to a stop with one wheel on the curb. She tried to draw air into her lungs but she was shaking so hard she couldn't even manage that.

"You're not going to faint on me, are you? I don't know CPR."

"What...how...I don't—"

His grin widened. "So you can finally see me. I was wondering if it would happen in time for the wedding."

Cautiously she extended a finger and poked his forearm. She'd half expected it to be like trying to poke a puff of smoke, but she encountered one-hundred-percent solid masculine muscle mass.

"Oh, my God!" She knew she should scream or faint or do whatever it was you were expected to do when reality runs right up against the impossible, but all she could do was stare at him. "Either you're the best magician in the universe or I'm seeing a ghost." She wasn't sure which alternative she preferred.

"I'm not a ghost."

The flutter in her chest testified to her relief. He was too glorious to be a ghost. Too big and male and powerful to be anything but flesh and blood—

"Wait a minute," she said as what remained of her rational mind kicked in. "This is a tiny car. How could you possibly—"

"I wasn't hiding. I'm invisible."

"Sure you are. And I'm Elvis Presley."

"You don't believe me."

"Damn right, I don't." She didn't know exactly what she believed at the moment, but she did know what she had to do. She pointed toward the passenger door. "Get out."

He shook his head.

"If you don't get out in ten seconds, I'll call the cops."

"You don't want to do that." The sparkle in his eyes was infuriating. "Nobody else can see me. Believe me, I've tried."

Her response was earthy.

"Nice talk," he said. "Somebody should wash your mouth out with soap."

She threw the VW into gear and roared into the street.

"Where are you going?"

"To the police station."

"You're only going to embarrass yourself."

"That's my business."

"They'll probably think you're drunk."

"I'm not drunk," she said through gritted teeth. "I never get drunk."

"You were drunk last night."

Again she brought the VW to a screeching halt. "What do you know about last night?"

A look of mock dismay creased his glorious features. "Forgot already, Jenna? I'm wounded. I'd always heard I was a pretty good kisser."

She grabbed him by the worn collar of his leather jacket. It felt warm and supple beneath her fingers, as real and tangible as her own silk shirt. *Hang onto that thought.* "I repeat, *what do you know about last night?*"

"This." He pulled her across his lap and before she could draw her next breath, his mouth claimed hers and she knew that nothing would ever be the same again.

Chapter Three

Chase was in trouble again, only this time it had
nothing to do with abandoned mines and legendary curses and everything to do with the woman
he held in his arms.

She was warm and soft, all ripe curves and
golden skin. Sweeter than the most exotic garden on
a summer's night. Her long dark hair drifted over
his arms as he held her, and he wondered how she
would look naked with only that banner of silk to
shield her from his eyes.

Her mouth opened on a gasp and he seized the
moment, same as he had less than twenty-four
hours ago. He knew he was confusing the issue,
that he didn't need to woo her in order to wed her,
but the pull was as irresistible as it was dangerous.

He knew the moment when shock turned to heat,
knew it by the way she melted against him, a soft
moan of pleasure sounding deep in her throat. He

captured that sound with his mouth, made it his own. He wanted to claim every beautiful inch of her body, taste the sweet honey between her thighs, bury his length inside her.

He'd wanted women before, wanted them as badly as he wanted Jenna Grey, but this was different, and it was that difference that should have warned him away.

JENNA KNEW this was madness, a walk on the wild side, but caution had vanished the moment his mouth claimed hers. Her hands slipped beneath his battered leather jacket, inched beneath the hem of his white T-shirt, slid along the rippling muscles of his abdomen. She kept her eyes tightly closed. She didn't need to see him at all. Her palms registered his heat and his hardness, registered the violent thudding of his heart.

She was vaguely aware of his hands cupping her breasts, of the rapid sound of his breathing, but all of her attention, her need, was concentrated on this erotic exploration of his body. She'd never hungered like this before, not for anything or anybody. It was a separate entity, this hunger. It devoured reason. How else could you explain what was happening between them?

Only madness even came close.

Desire turned her to flame. They were still fully clothed, but she found it difficult to tell where her body ended and his began. She'd always wondered what the fuss was about, why sane women danced on the edge of madness all for the touch of a man. Now she knew. And that knowledge made her feel invincible and vulnerable, wild and innocent.

Touching him was brand new...and strangely familiar. She knew the swell of each muscle, the long ridges of sinew, the woodsmoke and spice smell of his skin.

"Look at me," he commanded in a voice that rose from her darkest fantasies.

Slowly she lifted her lids, drinking in the angles and planes of his face.

And the high-beam flashlight that was pointed right at her.

"Oh, no!" She buried her face against Chase's shoulder, wishing she were invisible. *Now you've done it, Jenna.*

"Step outside, please."

She struggled to see what lay behind the glare. "Can you see who it is?" she asked Chase.

"I think it's the cops," he said, still holding her in his arms.

"We've asked you to step outside, miss."

She wondered why they were so concerned with her and not with the man in whose arms she was reclining, but chalked it up to the fact that she was the driver of the car.

"His hand's on his holster," Chase said. "Maybe you'd better get out."

Cheeks burning, she scrambled from the car, thanking the patron saint of libidinous women that her clothing was still where it should be.

Two policemen faced her. One held the flashlight beam on her face. The other held a gun.

"What on earth—?" She stared from one officer to the other. "I didn't do anything wrong." She paused. "Did I?"

"License and registration, please," said the officer with the gun.

"You're joking."

"No, ma'am, we're not joking."

She reached into the car and grabbed for her bag. "I can't believe this," she said to Chase as she fumbled for the documents. "I've never been pulled over before in my entire life."

"You weren't pulled over," he pointed out with a display of male logic at its most annoying. "You were already stopped."

She waved an impatient hand in the air. "Same difference."

One of the cops appeared next to her. "Who are you talking to, ma'am?"

She wanted to ask him if he was blind but thought better of it. After all, the man was carrying a weapon. "I'm talking to my friend."

The cop cast a look at his fellow officer. "Your friend?"

"Chase," she called out. "Why don't you introduce yourself?"

"I'm trying," said the magician, who was leaning against the side of the VW. "They're not listening."

"Try harder."

"Ma'am," said the taller of the cops. "Please place your hands on the roof of the vehicle."

"This is getting ridiculous," Jenna said, struggling to rein in her temper. "I haven't done anything wrong."

"We're not accusing you of anything, ma'am," the cop continued. "But we need to assess the situation."

"Assess the situation? What situation?" Quinn barked.

"Exactly," said Jenna. "What situation?"

The two oafs in uniform looked confused. She didn't know whether to laugh or cry.

"They can't see me," Quinn said.

"That's impossible," Jenna said.

"Look." He stepped in front of the officers and assumed a boxer's stance. "No reaction."

"Ma'am," said the cop, "assume the position."

She did, much to Quinn's amusement. One of the cops did a quick pat-down.

"Nothing," the cop said to his partner.

"I could have told you that," Jenna said, indignant that there had been any doubt.

The first cop handed her a strange contraption. She backed away. "What's that?"

"Breathalyzer, ma'am."

"I'm not drunk!"

"Yes, ma'am," said his partner, "and this is a fine way to prove it."

"Quit laughing," she snapped at Chase. "There's nothing funny about this."

"Ma'am," said the first cop, an odd expression on his face. "I'll ask you again. Exactly who are you talking to?"

"Go ahead," Chase said, eyes glittering with amusement. "Tell them. I dare you."

"I can't tell them," she snapped again. "They're not going to believe me."

The second cop's grip tightened visibly on the gun. "We understand, ma'am. Now the Breathalyzer, if you would."

She did.

"Negative alcohol content," the first cop said.

"I told you," Jenna said, perhaps a trifle smugly considering the situation.

"Are you taking any medication?" the second cop asked.

"Absolutely not."

"Recreational drugs?"

"Never!"

The two cops exchanged meaningful looks. "Any previous history of mental illness?"

"Previous is redundant in that sentence," she said before she could stop herself.

"Bad move," Chase groaned. "These guys mean business."

"Ma'am, you haven't answered the question."

"That was a stupid question," Jenna persisted as the last vestiges of sanity vanished. "How do you answer a question like that?"

"Okay," said the second cop. "Fun's over." He pulled a pair of handcuffs from his back pocket while the first cop removed her car keys from the ignition. "We're going to the station."

"Chase!" she cried. "Help me!"

He wanted to but he was invisible, not superhuman. Those guys were packing heat, and he wasn't about to spill invisible blood for anyone, not even the beauteous Ms. Grey.

"I'll come with you," he said, "but keep your mouth shut before they have you committed to a mental institution."

"I haven't done anything wrong," she wailed. "I demand the right to call my lawyer. Tell them, Quinn!"

The two cops exchanged meaningful looks. "You can call your lawyer as soon as we get to the station," said the older one.

She opened her mouth to speak, but Chase clamped a hand on her shoulder. "Don't," he warned. "You'll only get in deeper."

She looked like she was going to burst with indignation but she managed to keep her mouth shut until they reached the patrol car. The younger cop placed a hand on her head then directed her into the back seat.

"Ouch! That hurt."

"I didn't lay a hand on you, lady," the cop protested. "I kept you from bumping your head."

"Not you," she said. "He stepped on my foot."

"I wasn't anywhere near you," said the older cop. "I was climbing in the driver's side."

"Sorry," said Chase. "I had to squeeze in before he slammed the door on me."

"This isn't going to work," she said in a heated whisper. "You don't know how hard it is to remember you're invisible."

"Invisible?" The older cop swiveled around in his seat to stare at her. "Who's invisible?"

Chase had to hand it to her. She had the vacant stare down pat. "You must have misunderstood, Officer," she said. "I said, 'indivisible.'"

"That's worse," said the younger cop. "I don't even know what that word means."

"Don't push it," Chase warned. "These guys mean business."

"Indivisible," she said, a wicked gleam replacing the vacant stare. "Don't you know the Pledge of Allegiance? I'm speaking about my inalienable rights as a citizen to retain an attorney."

"Lady, we already told you you can call a lawyer. We don't have a problem with that."

"Fine," said Jenna, sitting back. "Just as long as we understand each other."

"Understand you?" Chase said with a laugh. "They're scared stiff of you."

"Me? Why would they be scared of me?"

"Because they think you're crazy."

"I'm not crazy. This situation is what's crazy—"

"Ma'am," said the younger cop. "We'll be at the station in a few minutes. Maybe you want to save your story for when we get there."

Her eyes slowly widened. "They really can't see you, can they?"

"They really can't see me."

"Oh, my God," she murmured, closing her eyes. One of them was crazy and she was no longer certain it wasn't her.

EVEN JENNA HAD TO ADMIT it looked pretty strange on paper.

"I can't sign this," she said, pushing the document back to Liz's husband, Frank. "This isn't the way it happened."

Frank, an attorney who kept non-Vegas hours, smothered a yawn. "There's nothing incriminating in this statement, Jenna. It's a verbatim transcript." He fiddled with his Mont Blanc fountain pen. "Unless you're telling me these aren't your words."

Jenna waved her hand in the air. "Oh, they're my words. I just didn't expect them to look so... weird."

"Trust me. This whole situation *is* weird."

"Well, it looks even weirder on paper." She fidgeted on the rickety wooden chair. "I'm not drunk, under the influence of drugs or mentally impaired. Why don't they let me go home?"

"They'll let you go home as soon as you sign this document for their files."

She made a face. "Look at this, Frank! It says I was lying across the front seat, talking to myself, and that I carried on an animated conversation with an empty car while the police were questioning me."

"You weren't lying across the front seat talking to yourself? You weren't talking to an empty car?"

She hesitated. How could she tell him the rest of the story? Frank would have her committed, and she wouldn't blame him. Especially now that Chase Quinn seemed to have once again vanished into thin air. She hadn't seen or heard a word from him since they arrived at the station house. Was it possible she'd imagined the whole thing? "I had a good reason."

"I'm too tired for reasons, Jenna. Just sign this and let's get out of here."

She became aware of the cops who were openly eavesdropping on the conversation. The last thing she needed was a reputation for flakiness that could derail her fledgling enterprise. "All right," she said, reaching for Frank's pen. "I'll sign."

"You won't regret it," Frank said, stifling another yawn as he snagged a glance at his watch.

She already did. There was something about seeing the story laid out there in black and white that made her face flame with embarrassment. Was she going crazy, she wondered as she signed her name in the appropriate places. Was she so pathetically starved for a man's touch that she'd conjured one up from the whole cloth of memory and desire?

She was a rational woman with a rational woman's take on life. Her car was roughly the size of a large can of peas. The odds of hiding a grown man in there were about a million to one. If there'd been someone in the VW with her, the police would have seen him. As it was, she was the only person the police had seen, all of which could mean just one thing.

She was losing her mind.

CHASE WATCHED the proceedings from the top of the filing cabinet across the room. He'd tried standing in the doorway but he got tired of being a crash wall for cops anxious to get a good look at Jenna. He hoped they weren't detectives. They'd bumped right into him and never once realized the difference between human flesh and a doorjamb.

Not that he could blame them for being distracted—she was one hell of a beautiful woman— but the rumor had gotten around that she was also crazy as a coot, and the combination had proven irresistible.

He had to hand it to her attorney. The guy was half-asleep but he still managed to stay on top of things, guiding Jenna through the maze of legal documents with dispatch.

"A chronological statement of fact *not* an admission of guilt..."

His foot tapped against the metal cabinet, and Jenna turned in his direction.

"Did you hear that?" she asked Frank.

The attorney shook his head. "The only thing I want to hear is the sound of my own snoring."

"I know I heard something." She tilted her head in Chase's direction. "It sounded like someone kicked the cabinet."

"You worry about the cabinet," said the attorney, glancing his way. "I'll worry about keeping you out of jail."

Chase listened as Frank described in detail the whys and wherefores of the documents Jenna had signed. A few times he waved at Jenna, but she didn't see a thing, which made him wonder about the rules of invisibility. Did it have something to do with the temperature or the humidity or was it tied up with a less predictable variable, like emotion? Sometimes she saw him, sometimes she didn't, and he couldn't find any logic to the whole thing.

Not that there was anything logical about curses, but it seemed to Chase that even the impossible had to be governed by some kind of laws, and if it wasn't, it should be.

He wondered how she'd feel about an invisible groom.

"I HAVE NEVER been more embarrassed in my entire life," Jenna stated as Frank led her down the front steps of the police station.

"Rule number one," said Frank. "Leave your imaginary friends at home."

"Very funny," Jenna said, shooting him a look. "I don't have an imaginary friend."

Frank stopped walking and placed a hand on her forearm. "Listen to me, Jenna. Cops tend to be short on imagination and long on reality. They don't have a lot of patience with flights of fancy."

"I'm not crazy, Frank."

"I never said you were."

"You don't have to. I can see it in your eyes."

"What you see is exhaustion." He glanced at his watch. "It's almost four in the morning and I have a deposition in less than five hours."

"Frank, I—" She stopped. What was the point? After the last three humiliating hours she should know better than to mention the words "invisible" and "man" in the same sentence.

She glanced at Frank. He was a solid, rational husband, father and lawyer. He believed in things he could see and hear and touch. Good grief, he didn't even read novels because he preferred reality to fantasy any day of the week. No wonder he wanted her to sign that paper and get out with the least amount of fuss.

You don't know the half of it, Frank, she thought. *I wasn't taking a catnap in the front seat. I was—* She stopped as a violent wave of pleasure spiraled through her midsection. Good thing the police showed up when they did. A few minutes later and they might have found her *en deshabille*... and all by herself.

A man disappears inside an abandoned mine then reappears two years later masquerading as a statue who sweeps her off her feet and into his arms. Then this disappearing man pops up in her Volkswagen where, in a fit of blind lust, she flings herself at him just in time to be arrested by the local police.

It could happen.

"I'll drive you back to get your car," Frank said, opening the passenger door of his midnight blue Cadillac.

She made a face. "I don't want to see my car," she said, settling herself down in the cushy leather interior. Maybe the darned thing was haunted. "I'll worry about my car tomorrow."

"It's no trouble."

"I've put you out enough, Frank. The car's on the other side of town."

Frank stifled a yawn. "Better now than later."

"Then I guess so."

"You're sure?"

She nodded. At the moment it was just about the only thing Jenna *was* sure about.

That and the fact that she wanted a man who wasn't there . . . and maybe never had been.

Chapter Four

"Get a good night's sleep," Frank said when he deposited Jenna at her car. "And don't talk to any invisible men."

"Very funny." She swatted him on the arm.

"Liz told me the hours you've been putting in for the opening. Slow it down, Jenna. You'll live longer."

She kissed his stubbly cheek. "Thanks again for the help. I really appreciate it."

"Just don't make a habit of it. Next time our friendly neighborhood police force might not be so understanding."

They won't have to be, Jenna thought as she climbed into the VW. There wouldn't be a next time. Frank was right. She'd been working too hard for too long and it had finally taken its toll on her sanity. Fatigue and champagne and loneliness all had conspired to conjure up a fantasy that had seemed more real than life itself.

But she was wise to it now. You couldn't get by on two hours' sleep a night for long and not pay the price. "Early to bed, early to rise," she said as she started the engine and adjusted her rearview mirror. Regular meals, daily exercise. That was the way to keep invisible lovers at bay.

The bright lights of the city faded in her rearview mirror, and she unrolled her window and took a deep breath. The air was sweet and clear, tinged with odd notes of wood smoke and spice, so different from the air she'd grown up with in Chicago, air that had been heavy with the smell of fear and despair. She'd been barely seventeen when she left her last foster family, slipping out in the middle of the night with only a small suitcase and her dreams. She knew she had to get away, had to find a life of her own, or she'd end up just like everyone else, dreaming of all the things that might have been.

That was almost ten years ago. Life had been very good to her, and if she hadn't found the husband and family she'd wished for, she had good friends and a promising future.

And a home she loved.

"I don't know why you wanted to buy way out here," Liz had said during Jenna's housewarming party last year. "It's in the middle of nowhere."

Jenna had just smiled. She knew that people laughed over the bland suburban sprawl of neat little houses on neat little plots of desert, but the moment she saw it, she felt like she'd come home for the very first time.

As she turned onto her street, she realized that the scent of wood smoke and spice was still present even though she'd rolled her window up against the cold. The scent was familiar, strangely so, but she couldn't quite place it.

She parked the car in the driveway and tilted her head, listening. She didn't know what she was listening for or why, but all her senses were suddenly on alert.

"Impossible," she said, her fingers curved around the wheel. The tick of the engine was a counterpoint to the thudding of her heart.

Her breath caught in her throat. The seat was squashed almost flat, as if someone was sitting on it.

"No!" The word exploded from her lips. "This is ridiculous." She wasn't going to let her imagination tie her up in knots again. She'd already made a fool of herself in front of Frank and half the local police force. That was more than enough for one night.

Turning off the engine, she grabbed her purse and leapt from the car.

"I'm crazy," she muttered, racing for the door. Certifiably, absolutely mad as a hatter. She was surprised she hadn't realized it sooner.

"Jenna."

His voice wrapped itself around her heart like a warm caress.

"No," she whispered, fitting the key into the lock with trembling fingers. The word was more a thought than a sound. "Go away."

"You don't want that," the smoke-and-brandy voice said as she flung the door open.

"Don't tell me what I want. You don't even exist. I'm talking to thin air." She burst into the house then made to slam the door shut. The door wouldn't budge.

"That's my foot," said the voice. "Now you can close it."

The door forgotten, she ran through the hallway, skidding on the slickly polished oak floor as she turned for the bedroom. She heard footsteps behind her, coming closer, faster. She burst into the bedroom and made to slam the door shut, as if a mere door could keep the demons at bay, but it wouldn't budge. She leaned into it with her shoulder and pushed with all her might, but moving Mount Rushmore would be easier.

"Where are you?" She fairly screamed the words. "What do you want from me?"

She felt his touch at her waist and a violent shock of recognition jolted through her body.

"I'm here," he said, his voice midnight and dark promises.

Tears welled, burning against her lids. "Don't do this to me. I can't— I don't understand."

"That makes two of us."

She pulled away, not knowing which way to run, not knowing what she was running from, only that if she stayed there a moment longer she'd never again draw a breath that wasn't somehow connected to him.

The scent of wood smoke and spice grew stronger. She sensed him before her, felt his heat, his power, but she couldn't see him. Terror nipped the length of her spine.

"Things like this don't happen," she whispered as she thought of his sad golden eyes, the proud line of his mouth, the—

Suddenly he stood before her, her deepest fantasy come to life right before her eyes. *Chase Quinn.* The lean, hard-muscled body. The snug jeans and battered leather jacket. The memory of his mouth on hers made her breath catch in her throat.

That strong mouth curved in a half smile. "I knew you could do it."

"I didn't do anything. I want you to go away and leave me alone."

"You see me, don't you, Jenna?"

She nodded, not trusting her voice.

"You're the only one who can."

"I don't want to see you. I've never wanted to see you. I want you to get out of my head and leave me alone!"

Was that a flicker of sadness she saw on his face, a touch of regret, or was she so far gone she couldn't tell a real man from a dream?

"I can't leave you alone. You're the only one who can help me."

"Why are you doing this to me?"

"Because you're the one who remembers."

She choked back a strangled laugh. "Remembers what?"

"Me."

"I don't know what you're talking about."

"The statue. That's what started this whole thing."

"What whole thing?" She was beginning to feel like a demented parrot.

"You're the one who brought me back."

"Where were you?" she asked, trying to ignore the fact that he seemed to be fading in and out right in front of her eyes.

"I don't know."

"You can do better than that." She inched her way toward the door. "Tahiti? The south of France? Pittsburgh?"

He grinned. "Pittsburgh sounds good."

"You're a magician," she said, getting closer to the door. "This must be some fancy sleight of hand."

"I'm good but I'm not *that* good."

"I know there's a rational explanation for all of this." She swallowed as his torso vanished then reappeared. "There has to be."

"You're not going to like it."

"What makes you think I've liked anything that's happened so far?"

Their eyes met and she remembered the warmth of his body against hers and every single deliciously decadent fantasy that warmth had conjured up.

There was only one thing left to do.

She ran for her life.

CHASE HAD SPENT his entire adult life turning away marriage-minded women by the dozen. Now that he was ready to take the plunge, the woman in question acted as if he'd suggested a long walk across a bed of burning coals.

Not that it couldn't be done. You could walk on burning coals, break bricks with your forehead, make an eighty-story building disappear, all with a wave of your hand. He'd learned you could do just about anything if you put your mind to it—and if you couldn't do it, you could make people think you had, which sometimes was even better.

That's what magic was really all about. Part reality, part illusion, and you counted on the illusion to carry you through to where you needed to be.

And right now he needed to be at the altar.

"You're making this hard, Jenna." He tackled her by the waist just two feet from the front door. "It's not like I'm asking you to do something illegal."

"Right," she said, struggling against him. "You only want to marry me."

"I'm not talking long-term commitment. We grab one of your preachers, say I do, then I'm out of here." What in hell was her problem, anyway? You'd think the fact that he was invisible would be upsetting her more than his proposal.

"Wow," she drawled. "Sweep me off my feet, why don't you?" They were eye to eye and she refused to look away. She was bright, beautiful and stubborn as a mule. Good thing he wasn't in love with her. This woman could be the death of him.

"Gimme a break, lady." He set her down. "I'm fighting for my life here."

"A trifle melodramatic, wouldn't you say?"

"Listen to me." He grabbed her by the shoulders, acutely aware of the delicacy of her bones, the softness of her skin, the way her perfume seemed to dance in the space between them. "I'm running out of time. If I don't get married by Sunday, I'm gone."

She burned with anger but instead of overpowering her beauty, it rendered her luminous.

Oh, yeah. A magnificent, *dangerous* woman.

"Wonderful," she said, beaming him a show-girl smile. "Be sure to send me a postcard from Pittsburgh."

"Damn it to hell!" Didn't she understand what he was talking about? "I'm not hopping a Greyhound, Jenna. I mean I'll be *gone.*"

Her eyes widened. "Gone as in dead?"

"That's what the man said."

"Man?" Her eyes widened some more. "What man?"

Good going, moron. She already thinks you're crazy. How do you explain this one to her?

"Chase." Her voice slid up an octave. "You're not talking about...God, are you?"

"No." He lowered his voice. "I don't think I can explain it to you without you getting scared."

"I'm already scared out of my mind," she said, yet to Chase she looked anything but. She looked like an Amazon warrior ready to do battle.

A gutsy, spectacular woman.

He sensed she wasn't going to run. At least not at the moment. Curiosity had got the better of her. He felt like a male Scheherazade, delaying his demise by spinning tales.

"I'm waiting," she said.

"I'm cursed."

Her full and beautiful mouth twitched. "You're cursed?"

"Yeah," he said, daring her to laugh at him. "I'm cursed."

"Uh-huh." Her lips began the subtle curve upward. "What happened? Wake up on the wrong side of your magic wand?"

"Go ahead," he said, dragging a hand through his hair in agitation. "Get it over with. Laugh if you want to."

"I don't want to laugh."

"The hell you don't." He couldn't stop staring at her perfect mouth, the swell of her lower lip, the definition of the upper.

"You have to admit it isn't every day a man tells a woman he's cursed."

"Damn right I'm cursed. Why else would I want to get married?"

"People get married for a lot of reasons," she retorted. "Sometimes they're actually in love."

"You don't buy that any more than I do."

"You don't know the first thing about me, Chase Quinn. Don't go telling me what I think."

He lifted her left hand. "No rings. No fiancé. No husband." He dropped her hand. "Case closed."

"The case is not closed." Her anger was even more amazing than he'd imagined it would be. The silken mane of dark hair seemed to crackle around her slender shoulders and beautiful face. Her turquoise eyes were fierce with emotion. "I know your type, Quinn. You use that fallen angel face of yours to lull women into a false sense of security, then as soon as you get what you want, you're onto your next victim. You can just count me out."

Suddenly it all made sense to him and he wondered why he hadn't caught on sooner. "Don't take it out on me because some stupid s.o.b. dumped you."

Her right hand balled into a fist, and he ducked just in time to save his jaw.

"Damn," he said, shaking his head. "You could hurt a guy with a punch like that."

"My love life is none of your business," she said through clenched teeth.

"So you have a love life." He glanced around the room, taking inventory. "I was beginning to wonder."

"I repeat, my love life is none of your business."

"Of course, there are two ways to look at this," he continued, relishing the fire in her eyes. "Either you're beating the guys off with a stick, or you're all talk and no action. Either way I can handle it."

"Handle it?" Her voice rose yet another octave. "*Handle it?* One more word like that and you'll be handling it from intensive care."

"When was the last time you went out on a date?"

"I'm not answering that."

"Yeah, and I know why. It's been so long you probably can't remember."

"I can so remember."

"So when was it?"

She glanced away for a moment. "A few weeks ago."

"Weeks?"

"You don't have to sound so suspicious."

"You don't have to lie."

"Okay, so it was last year. Big deal. Dating is highly overrated." She aimed another of those high-voltage dirty looks in his direction. "And don't tell me that's because I haven't dated you."

"Ouch," he said wincing. "Do you really think I'd use a worn-out line like that?"

"Yes," she said. "I do."

"Give me credit for some originality."

"I'm not going to give you credit for anything," she shot back. "I just want you out of my house."

"We need to talk."

"We have nothing to talk about."

"There's the future to consider."

"Believe me, we have no future."

"Seems to me I'm exactly the kind of guy you should get involved with."

"You're invisible."

"So what?"

She blinked, almost as if she were rousing from a dream. "I can't believe we're even having this conversation. I'm a rational, intelligent human being. I know there has to be an explanation for all of this."

"I gave you the explanation," he said, beginning to grow exasperated. "I'm cursed."

"That's what you want me to believe," she said. "Now tell me what *you* believe."

"I believe it. And I believe you're my last chance."

"I don't want to be your last chance," she said, the dangerous fire back in her turquoise eyes. "I don't want to be anything to you. I just want you to go away and leave me alone."

"You should have thought of that before you made that statue of me."

"I made a statue of Cleopatra and you don't see her in my kitchen doing the dishes. Statues are statues. You—" she poked him in the chest "—are something else."

"Is that a compliment?"

She poked him again. "You obnoxious pig!"

"Yeah, it's a compliment," he said, grinning as they returned to familiar territory. "That statue nailed me right down to my—"

"Don't even say it," she warned. "That statue was a product of my imagination."

"And a damn good imagination it is. How did you know that my—"

"I guessed."

"Good guess."

Was he imagining it or did a wicked smile hover just beneath the surface? "I might have been a bit...generous in one area."

"Dead on," he said, enjoying the sparks jumping between them. "You're good with your hands."

"So are you."

"How would you know?"

"I saw your act once. I was between shows and I watched from backstage. I was wearing the cornucopia on my head for the Hooray for Autumn show. You sawed Wayne Newton in half. The audience hated me, loved you."

"Hard to believe I didn't notice you."

"You were too busy noticing Yvette and Sandy and Leila—want me to go on? Your reputation precedes you."

"Don't believe everything you hear."

She started to laugh. "If I believed everything I'd heard about you, we wouldn't be standing here having this conversation. I'd be calling the *Guinness Book of World Records*."

"So why *are* we having this conversation?"

She hesitated and he saw a flicker of doubt in her eyes. "I don't know," she said. "Maybe I'm trying to make sense out of an impossible situation."

"It's not impossible," he said. "Just unlikely."

"How do I know this isn't some elaborate publicity stunt?"

"You don't."

She reached out and placed her hand against his chest. Her touch seemed to sizzle through flesh and bone, straight to the heart he'd never believed he possessed. *Why her? Why now?* This whole thing was complicated enough. He didn't need emotion to get in there and make it worse.

"You're not a figment of my imagintion," she said slowly. "I can touch you. I can smell your cologne. I can hear you speak. I can see you and—"

She looked away.

"You tasted like coffee and raspberries." His words filled the silence. They were the wrong words. They were the kind of words that got a man in trouble. But they were the only words that would do. "The inside of your mouth was hot and sweet."

IT WAS a full frontal assault, setting the fight-or-flight response into motion. She'd already tried the latter and failed. Maybe the former would be her salvation.

"Get lost!" She poked him in the chest, trying to ignore the fact that it was a very *nice* chest. Thinking about his torso was only going to get her in trouble and she already had more than enough of that commodity to last a lifetime. "If I brought you here, I can send you away." She snapped her fingers right under his nose. "Scat!"

"Scat?" He moved closer. "It didn't work."

"I noticed."

"What next?"

She glanced toward her nightstand. "Mace?"

"Not a great idea."

"There has to be some way to make you leave."

"There is," he said, his golden eyes sparkling. "You can marry me."

She couldn't help herself. She hauled off and delivered a roundhouse punch to his stomach.

The rat didn't even blink. "Was that a yes or a no?"

"Marry you? I don't even know who you are." Her laugh bordered on hysteria. "I don't even know *what* you are."

He bowed from the waist, a perfect parody of polite behavior. She felt like punching him again but figured that might be pressing her luck. "I'm the man you're going to marry."

"Stop saying that!" She glared at him. "There's no way that's going to happen."

"It's going to happen."

"Not in this lifetime."

"You don't seem to get it, Jenna. I'm not going anywhere until you say you'll marry me. I'll be here when you go to sleep. I'll be here when you wake up in the morning. I'll hand you the soap when you take your shower and watch you blow dry your hair and pour the milk on your cornflakes and—"

Her scream of frustration was shrill enough to break glass. "No! Never! No way! Absolutely positively not in this lifetime or any other!"

"Great," he said with a satisfied grin. "You'll think about it."

Chapter Five

"Out!" She pointed toward the door. "Now!"

"You're being hasty. We need to talk about this."

"I'm not talking to you about anything. Get out!"

"Maybe I didn't phrase it right," he said, regrouping. "I want a wedding. I don't want a marriage." He shot her a Kodachrome smile. "Is that better?"

"Better? You're the most insulting excuse for a man I've ever met in my entire life." She placed her hands on his chest and pushed. "I'm going to get you out of here if I have to hire a tow truck to *pull* you out."

"You have one hell of a temper, lady," he said, his good humor fading.

"You bring out the best in me." She glanced around the room until her eyes lighted on the stand near the door.

"No weapons," he said. "Let's keep it clean."

She ignored him and grabbed for the bright red golf umbrella. "Get out!"

He ducked. "You could poke someone's eye out with that thing."

"I'll poke more than your eye if you don't get out by the time I count to three."

"What the hell have I done wrong?"

"One..."

"All I did was ask you to marry me."

"Two..."

"It's not like I want to sleep with you."

She lifted the umbrella and made to bring it crashing down over his head, but before she could make contact with his skull he vanished.

"Hey!" she called out. "Come back here. You don't just disappear in the middle of a conversation."

"That wasn't a conversation. That was assault and battery."

"I didn't lay a hand on you."

"You were about to."

"I was not."

His voice came from behind her. "You wouldn't say that if we had an instant replay."

She spun around, umbrella still poised, but saw nothing. "This isn't funny. Undo whatever you just did."

"I'm telling you I didn't do a damn thing. I don't know why you can't see me."

She spun to her right. "Stop moving around! This is weird enough as it is. The least you can do is stay in one place."

"Are you always this bossy or do you save this routine for all your future husbands?"

She swung out with the back of her hand and was rewarded with a yelp from Chase.

"Another shot like that and there won't be a honeymoon," he said in a tone approaching a growl.

"I didn't hit you that hard," she protested, feeling moderately guilty but not enough to apologize.

"Your aim made up for it."

"If you'd go back where you came from, maybe you wouldn't have these problems."

"That's it, lady. You finally convinced me. I'd rather stay invisible."

She heard the sound of footsteps marching down the hallway toward the front door. She took a step forward to go after him, then stopped abruptly, her heart beating furiously inside her chest. What was the matter with her? He was leaving. That's what she wanted, wasn't it?

She wrapped her arms about her chest and waited for the sound of the door opening then closing again. She heard the familiar squeak of the hinges, a small thud as the door hit the doorstop, then a string of inventive curses that boggled the mind.

Astonished, she stepped into the hallway. The door was wide open. A spill of moonlight puddled on the shiny wood floor.

"I'm trapped," Chase said in a voice of doom.

"Don't be ridiculous. The door's wide open."

"I can't step over the doorjamb."

"Try harder! You can't stay here."

She heard a slight scuffle, a bump, then another colorful string of phrases guaranteed to earn a page in her book of memories.

"I can't believe this," she said, agitation rising. She'd finally convinced him to leave and now her own house wouldn't cooperate. "Try the window." He had to go. She didn't trust herself alone in the house with him. He was everything she didn't like in a man, but somehow he made her feel more alive than she'd ever felt before.

She followed his footsteps into the living room and watched, astonished, as one of the side windows seemed to rise of its own accord.

"What's all this junk on the windowsill?"

Her plants went skittering to the floor in a flurry of pebbles and potting soil.

"My African violets!" She bent down quickly to right them. "How dare you toss my African violets around like that?"

"What if you had a fire? It would take you ten years to climb out over the crap you've got lined up."

"It's a security measure," she said. "It's a well-known fact that burglars pick houses with easy access."

"Right," said her invisible intruder. "And cutesy flowers on the windowsill will keep them out."

She picked up a clod of dirt and threw it in what she hoped was his direction. "It slowed you down, didn't it?"

"Not for long."

She heard a scuffling nose, the scrape of shoe leather against wood, then nothing.

"Are you out?" she asked.

"It's like trying to break through concrete," he said, sounding more disgusted than before.

She walked over to the window and extended her hand through the opening. "I can do it."

She heard a thud then another muttered curse. "I think I broke my hand."

"You can't break your hand on an open window."

"You cañ't talk to an invisible man but you're doing it."

She hesitated. "You have a point."

He closed the window again. "Do you have sliding doors?"

She nodded. "In the dining room."

They slid open like a charm, but again no dice.

"I can't believe this," she said from the deck outside. "I'm not having a problem."

Bathroom, bedroom, den, all with no luck.

"The basement," she said, brightening. "There's a window in there."

"I hate basements," he said. "Too damn dark."

"Seems to me you don't have much of a choice."

She led him down the wooden stairs that led to the crowded storage area. "Way back there." She pointed toward a window near the hot water heater. "That's the easiest one to open."

His footsteps sounded angry. She could just imagine what his face looked like. "Good riddance," she muttered as the window slid open. She liked her life exactly the way it was, thank you very much, and she certainly didn't need someone like Chase Quinn turning it all on its ear. He made her feel crazy and out of control, more like a love-starved teenager with the common sense of a fruit fly than a rational adult woman who should have learned better.

The window slid shut with a bang.

Her heart leapt inside her chest.

"Quinn?" She stepped closer. "Are you still here?"

"You could break out of Alcatraz faster than this place."

She jumped at the sound of his voice next to her right ear. "Try again. This just doesn't make sense."

"Hey, lady, nothing's made sense since the day I walked into that damn mine."

"That's not my problem," she snapped. "I just want you out of my house." She knew exactly what would happen if he stayed. The chemistry between them was too powerful, too intense to be denied, and she knew there was only one place where it could lead. "You find a way out and I'm history."

"There has to be some way to get you out of here," she said, desperate to put as much space as possible between herself and temptation.

"There is," he said grimly. "Marriage."

HE WAS a persuasive debater, but Jenna wouldn't give an inch except at daybreak when she finally gave in to exhaustion.

"I'm going to bed," she said to Chase who was now half-visible and trying to pry his way out of the living room window. "You do whatever you want. I'm too tired to care."

"Bed sounds good," he said, rising to his feet. How he could move so easily in those skin-tight jeans was beyond her. But then just about everything was beyond her at the moment. This whole situation was so bizarre that it was almost laughable. *Almost.*

"Where do you think you're going?" she demanded, hands on her hips.

"To bed." That fallen angel face managed to look quite innocent.

She pointed toward the couch. "There's your bed."

"Too short," he said. "I'll never fit."

"That's your problem."

"You're a cruel woman, Jenna Grey. Anybody ever tell you that?"

"No," she said, stifling a yawn. "Can't say that they have. Actually I'm quite proud of myself." For a woman known for picking up strays of both the two-and four-legged variety, this was quite a turnaround.

"So you're just going to go off to bed and leave me here?"

"That's the plan."

"What about a toothbrush?"

"I'll find you one."

"A pillow?"

"In the hall closet."

"A blanket?"

"Same place."

"Gonna tuck me in?"

"Don't push it," she warned.

His laughter followed her into her bedroom and seeped beneath the door when she closed it. She stared at the lock for a second. She'd never used it

before but it didn't seem a bad idea to do so tonight.

CHASE HAD NEVER HAD a bedroom door locked on
him before. A few women had tried to lock him in,
but as far as he could remember, Jenna was the first
one to lock him out. Under different circumstances he might have found it a challenge. This
time it was just an unnecessary roadblock.

Damn the woman. Why couldn't she get it
through her head that he wasn't interested in her
body—delectable though it might be. He was interested in her hand in marriage. Five minutes of
her time, that's all he was asking for. Five minutes
and she'd never have to see his face again as long as
she lived.

That wasn't such an unreasonable thing to ask
for. Hell, a bad date took up twenty times that or
more. As far as he was concerned she could sign the
marriage document with one hand and file the annulment papers with the other. He didn't care. All
he cared about was breaking the curse and reclaiming his life.

She wasn't this way with her friends. He'd seen
the way she walked around like Las Vegas's answer
to Mother Teresa, dispensing wisdom and warm
hugs to every lost or confused soul to cross her
path. You'd think she'd be able to spare one or two
for him. It wasn't every day you met a man with a

curse on his head. Whatever happened to compassion?

JENNA WAS FEELING anything but compassionate. She stood by her locked door, listening for signs of activity from the rest of the house. Didn't men usually make more noise than that when they were stomping around? There was something unnerving about a quiet man . . . and something downright disturbing about a quiet man who was also invisible.

What if he's not out there?

"He's out there," she muttered. "He has to be out there."

If he wasn't out there, that meant he was in the bedroom with her, and that thought was enough to make her consider leaping out the window and head screaming for Lake Mead.

"Are you in here?"

No response.

"Chase!" She raised her voice a decibel. "Are you in this room?"

Still no response.

She extended her arms and paced the length of the room. If he was anywhere in the vicinity, she was bound to bump into him, but the only thing she tripped over was a bunny slipper in the middle of the room. Satisfied—at least somewhat—she drew her nightgown from the middle drawer of her lingerie bureau.

Long.

White.

One-hundred-percent cotton.

She grinned as she draped it over her shoulder and headed for the master bath. If he was watching her, he was in for a major disappointment.

CHASE SPRAWLED on the sofa and listened to the sound of water running from the bathroom in the back of the house. It had been running for at least twenty minutes, and he figured the odds were she was taking a bath.

Which meant she was naked.

Given the spectacular way she looked in her clothes, naked had to be lethal. Back when he worked the Paradise Hotel, he'd seen more than his share of show girls in varying stages of undress. After awhile even the healthiest of red-blooded American men grew jaded at the sight of high, full breasts and long, willowy legs and faces that could launch a thousand ships.

Jenna Grey had all of those attributes and more. That long silky dark hair. The bright turquoise blue eyes. Peaches-and-cream skin that was probably flawless everywhere.

It didn't get much better . . . or more tempting.

And he didn't need to be tempted. Temptation was how he'd gotten into this mess in the first place. If he'd been able to resist pulling that stunt in the Tucker Mine, none of this would have happened. He'd be back centerstage at the big room at the Paradise, basking in the applause...wondering why it wasn't enough.

He sat up, annoyed by the turn his fantasy had taken. He'd never needed anything more than the adulation tumbling over the footlights. Or if he had, he'd been too busy to notice it.

No, it was something about this woman that was getting under his skin and had been from the first moment he saw her. It was part lust. Which was okay. Lust he understood. It was the other part, the unexplainable part, that rattled his cage. She touched him in a way no other woman had ever touched him, in a place no other woman had even thought to find.

Maybe it was the shadows drifting behind her keen blue eyes or the touch of sadness that made her beautiful face into something unforgettable. Or maybe it was the knowledge that of all the women in the world this was the one who could banish the demons.

He didn't know what it was. Hell, he didn't even want to know. All he wanted was to get his life back, that imperfect life that he understood, and get as far away from here as possible.

JENNA SLEPT SITTING UP with a flashlight in her right hand and a baseball bat in her left. She didn't know what good either would be against an invisible man but it was the best she could do under the circumstances. It wasn't that she expected him to come bursting through the door in a mad rage or anything, but she'd always believed it better to be safe than sorry.

Not that she felt safe or sorry at the moment. Mostly she felt a keen exhilaration that made her feel more alive than she had in years. The kind of alive that made your nerve endings tingle and the blood rush to your head and reminded you of what an adventure living could be.

The truth was, she couldn't remember the last time she felt exactly this way. Expectant, vibrant, alive to possibilities she couldn't name but knew were waiting for her just out of reach.

You're a sucker for trouble, Jenna. This man is too dangerous even for you.

So what if he was the most glorious man she'd ever seen in her life. So what if the loneliness in his golden eyes had found its mark deep in her heart. She'd made more than her share of mistakes when it came to men and been lucky enough to escape without permanent damage.

She doubted she'd be that lucky with Chase Quinn.

Heat rose from the soles of her feet, and she pressed her eyes closed against the erotic sensual memory of his kiss. *Too much,* she thought, placing a hand against her cheek. *Too fast.* She wasn't the kind of woman who threw herself into the arms of a stranger, caution and common sense be damned. Always she withheld a part of herself, as if she was waiting for a sign to tell her it was all right to open up her heart.

But not with Chase. Not even for a moment. There'd been no core of resistance inside her, no holding back. If he had pressed his advantage, she would have gone to him willingly.

It occurred to her that that was the difference between Chase and the other men in her life. The other men had always come to her on the rebound with badly broken hearts and damaged egos, and she'd soothed and nurtured and mothered them until they turned around and left her for another woman who didn't do any of those things.

There was nothing wrong with Chase's ego and she doubted he harbored a broken heart. She was fairly certain his heart had never even entered into most of the relationships he'd enjoyed with women. And she doubted he wanted soothing, nurturing or mothering from her or any other woman.

No, she thought as she lay there alone in bed, it was something darker. Something more disturbing and elemental that was at play here. That primal call of the blood between a man and woman that transcended every barrier civilization could erect between them. It was almost as if they were somehow fated to be together, and all the fighting in the world wouldn't change it.

Chapter Six

Thursday

Jenna dozed fitfully, starting awake at every odd noise. Finally, a little after eight o'clock in the morning, she gave up trying to sleep and climbed out of bed.

"You're a jerk," she said as she slipped into a pair of chestnut-brown trousers and a cream-colored sweater. Midnight thoughts, that's all they'd been. The kind of melancholy musings everyone entertained in the dark of night.

The sun was shining. The birds were singing. It was a new day, and she wasn't about to spend any more of it with her invisible houseguest than absolutely necessary.

Squaring her shoulders, she set out to do battle.

"Morning," Chase said as Jenna entered the kitchen. "Feel like breakfast?"

"My God!" She stopped dead in her tracks and stared at him. "You're naked!"

He glanced down. "Yeah."

"You can't be naked."

His grin was lazy and insolent both. "Why not?"

"This is a kitchen."

"You can't be naked in the kitchen?"

"You're frying bacon, for heaven's sake! You could . . . hurt something."

"I didn't know you cared." He flashed her a smile. "I'm wearing an apron."

It was quite obvious to anyone with decent vision that the apron was inadequate for the job.

"Put some clothes on."

"Can't," he said, turning the strips of smoked cholesterol.

"Of course you can." He took them off; he could put them back on again.

"They're in the washer."

"What are they doing in the washer?"

"This is a game, right?" He cracked three eggs into the skillet and slid them up against the bacon. "I say something, then you turn it into a question."

"I repeat, what are your clothes doing in the washer?"

"I've been in them for two years, Jenna. Figure it out."

"That's no excuse for nudity." *Listen to you, Jenna! You sound like a prudish schoolmarm.* Unfortunately she also felt like one at the moment. Unexpected male nudity was difficult to contend with at such an early hour. Especially in the kitchen.

Especially when you could look but not touch.

"I checked the hall closet. No men's stuff tucked away in there."

"A gentleman would wrap a towel around his middle."

His laughter bounced off the cabinets. "I've been called a lot of things, lady, but gentleman isn't one of 'em."

"Very original," she drawled, "but I think John Wayne said it before you."

"How do you like your eggs?"

"Clothed."

He stopped swishing the yellow mess around in the pan and turned to face her. "What's this hang-up with clothing, anyway?"

"It's not a hang-up," she said, pouring herself a glass of orange juice from the container sitting on the counter. "This isn't a nudist colony, it's my home, and most of my visitors keep their pants on."

He laughed again, louder this time.

"Poor choice of words," she mumbled into her juice glass. "You know what I mean."

"If you've got this problem with naked men, why didn't you put clothes on my statue?"

She choked on her juice. "That's hardly the same thing."

"Same body," he pointed out, quite unnecessarily. "What's the big deal?"

"It's just . . . different."

"How is it different?"

"It just is."

"Explain it to me," he persisted. "I really want to know."

She sighed in exasperation. "For one thing the statue doesn't talk."

"I'll stop talking."

"Too late," she said, reaching for a strip of bacon in the frying pan. "You can't turn back the game clock."

He yelped then slapped at his left thigh with his right hand. "Damn! You were right about frying bacon."

"I thought so," she said, as the minuscule apron revealed an important part of his anatomy. "I'll go get you a towel." *Or a tarp, as the case may be.*

Seconds later she returned with a huge pale pink bath sheet with her initials embroidered on the edge. She found him sitting—naked, of course—at the kitchen table, happily eating bacon and eggs as if he hadn't a care in the world.

"Here," she said, thrusting the towel in his direction and averting her eyes. "Put this on."

He thrust it back toward her. "It's pink."

"So what?"

"I don't wear pink."

"Oh, please." She rolled her eyes. "How absurd."

"Call it whatever you want to, but that doesn't change the facts. I'm not wearing pink."

"Pink isn't the first step on the road to a sex change operation," she pointed out with perhaps a touch more malice than the situation warranted.

"I don't give a damn if it's the first step on the road to the White House. I'm not wearing it."

"You're acting like a child."

He speared a huge chunk of egg with his fork. "So sue me."

"If I can't get you out of here soon, it might come to that."

He speared a piece of bacon. "Maybe we should put our heads together and come up with a solution."

"Get dressed," she said, turning away, "and we'll talk about it."

"You know what they say," he called after her as she fled. "If you can't stand the heat, stay out of the kitchen."

"Jerk," she muttered, storming into the laundry room. "Who in his right mind fries bacon stark naked?"

"You'd be hell on a camping trip. Probably keep your underwear on when you took a bath."

She checked the timer on the dryer. Still eight minutes to go. "People don't take baths on camping trips." She hesitated. "Do they?"

"Lady, you have a lot to learn."

"I don't go camping," she said stiffly. "How am I supposed to know?"

"I can see why you don't go camping. Holiday Inn is probably your idea of roughing it."

"Jerk," she said, to his face this time. "You don't know the first thing about me."

He lounged against the doorjamb. The apron around his midsection shifted a tad but not enough to cause him any embarrassment. Assuming, of course, the man was capable of being embarrassed.

"I think I like you better when you're invisible."

His left eyebrow lifted. "I didn't think you liked me at all."

"I don't," she said. "That was just a figure of speech."

"Too bad. It helps if you like the guy you're going to marry."

Her temper flared. "Get this straight, mister. I'm not going to marry you."

"This isn't my idea," he said. "I'm cursed, remember?"

She pushed past him and stormed into the kitchen. "And marriage is the curse?"

"Invisibility's the curse."

"You are one very strange man. How can marriage break a curse?"

"Simple," he said, reclaiming his seat at the kitchen table. "It's the last thing I want so it's the first thing I have to do."

"I know there's logic in there somewhere but I can't find it."

"Doesn't much matter if you can find it or not. Curses aren't logical."

"Well, find yourself another wife because I have no intention of marrying you."

"Sorry." He polished off the last of his toast. "It has to be you."

"Says who?"

He looked up at her, all wide-eyed innocence. "Actually, says you."

"Not in this lifetime."

"The way I heard it, I was in suspended animation until you created that statue of me."

"I don't understand."

"As close as I can tell, that called me back from wherever I was."

"Right," she said, nodding as if this all made perfect sense. "And because of the statue, I have to marry you."

"Now you get it." He looked inordinately pleased.

"You must have left a string of broken hearts a mile long, Quinn. Why don't you ask one of your old girlfriends to marry you?"

"Because you got there first."

She frowned, remembering. "Now wait a minute. You've been gone for almost two years. Are you telling me not one of them was pining away for you?"

"Not the way you were."

"I wasn't pining away for you," she pointed out, feeling the pinch of embarrassment. "All I did was make a statue."

"And the rest," he said, grinning, "was history."

The telephone cut off a biting retort.

"Where are you, girl?" Liz demanded. "After last night, I was afraid you'd headed for the hills."

"I'm running late," Jenna said, glancing at the clock over the sink. "Be there as soon as I can."

"Friend checking up on you?" Chase asked when she hung up.

"She's not checking up. She's concerned."

"That's the one who's married to the lawyer, right?"

Jenna nodded, gulping down her juice. "Not that it's any of your business."

"Always helps to know your wife's friends."

She wheeled to face him. "If you call me that one more time, so help me I'll stuff you back in that mine with my own bare hands." From the laundry room came the buzz of the dryer. "Your clothes are ready."

"You sound disappointed."

"What I sound is relieved."

He got up and headed for the laundry room. "Hey," he called out. "Do you have cable?"

She poked her head into the room, saw what he was doing, then turned away. The man definitely had a body to die for. "You're not planning on staying here, are you?"

"Remember last night? Doesn't look like I have much of a choice."

The phone rang again. "Liz," she said, by way of greeting, "I'm on my way. I swear to you!" But it wasn't Liz. In fact, she had no idea who it was. The line was open but her caller wasn't speaking. "This isn't a good day for fun and games. If you have something to say, say it or I'm hanging up."

"If it's for me, take a message," Chase called from the other room.

She waited a second then slammed down the phone.

"I can't believe this," Jenna mumbled, heading toward the hall closet. "This is a bad dream." It was like having a reprobate second cousin twice removed come to visit and refuse to leave. Well, maybe a second cousin twice removed *by marriage*. The emotions he brought to life inside her were anything but familial.

Which was another good reason for putting as much distance between them as possible.

She grabbed her bag, her jacket, then opened the front door, but when she tried to step outside it was like trying to walk through a brick wall. Her heartbeat accelerated. She stepped back, squared her shoulders, then gave it another go. "Ouch!" She bent down to rub her banged knee. "This is ridiculous!"

"Problem?" Chase popped up behind her.

"I can't get out."

"Welcome to the club."

"You don't understand. I *have* to get out. I have a business to run."

"I'm not stopping you."

"The hell you're not!" She reached out into space and rapped her knuckles against...something. "Plain, ordinary air doesn't sound like that."

"Tell me about it. I'm the one who was butting up against it last night."

"This is all your fault," she said, glaring at him. "Why couldn't you have just stayed out of that stupid mine in the first place?"

"Trust me, lady, if I'd known what I was getting myself into, I would have."

"So what are we going to do about it?"

"Beats me."

"We're prisoners," she said in despair. "Trapped like rats."

"Speak for yourself."

"I'm speaking for us. You got me into this mess and I think you should get me out of it."

"I don't know any more about curses than you do."

"Damn!" she whispered, gazing longingly at the world outside her door. On impulse she tried one more time to step over the threshold and was amazed to find herself successful. A second later she was even more amazed to find Chase standing next to her. "What on earth—"

"That's it," he said, looking toward the house. "It takes two of us to make it work."

"Great," she said, pulling the door closed and locking it. "I always wanted to be one of the Bobbsey Twins."

"You have a lousy attitude," Chase said as he followed her to her car. "Anybody ever tell you that?"

"As a matter of fact, no."

"Could've fooled me."

She opened the driver's side door. "Don't even think of coming with me. I'm washing my hands of you." She climbed inside. So did Chase. "You're not very bright, are you?" She started the engine. "Go find someone else to haunt."

"I'm not a ghost," he corrected her. "I'm just invisible."

"*Just* invisible," she said with an almost hysterical laugh. "Isn't that like being a little bit pregnant?"

"Are you?" he asked.

"Am I what?"

"Pregnant."

"No, I'm not pregnant," she said through gritted teeth.

"You still don't get it, do you? We're in this together."

"I must have been a serial murderer in another life." She backed down the driveway and onto the street. "That's the only answer I can come up with." Why else would she be punished this way?

"Cold," he said, looking at her. "Real cold. I have feelings, you know."

"I have an idea," she said, braking for a tortoiseshell cat ambling across the road. "Why don't I take you back to the mine and you can start all over again? I'm sure one of your many female admirers would be more than happy to take over where I left off.''

''I don't like this any better than you do, lady, but the way I see it we're stuck with each other.''

She angled him a look. '''Stuck' being the operative word.''

They drove the rest of the way to Fantasy Weddings in silence.

It occurred to Chase as he followed her into the back entrance to the building that beautiful women often had lousy personalities. Of course in Jenna's case that might be judging her too harshly. Under normal circumstances she might actually be a pleasant enough woman, but he hadn't seen evidence of that side of her yet.

''Just stay out of my way,'' she ordered as they walked down the hall toward her office. ''Go sit in the chapel or something but keep out of my sight.''

He grinned. ''So you do have a sense of humor after all.''

She wanted to smile. He could see the subtle movement at the corners of her mouth, but she managed to hold it back. *Too bad,* he thought. She had a spectacular smile and he wouldn't have minded basking in its glow.

''Jenna!'' The attorney's wife galloped after them. ''I thought I heard the VW outside. Where—'' She skidded to a stop at Jenna's side. ''You're wearing *that?*''

Jenna looked at her brown trousers, silk shirt and tailored blazer. "What's wrong with what I'm wearing?"

"It's so...so..."

"Conservative?" Chase supplied.

Jenna refused to meet his eyes. "Conservative?" she asked.

"Boring," said Liz.

"Boring's good," said Jenna. "Why should I get all dressed up just so I can change into my sweats and work in the studio?"

Liz looked as if she'd like to strangle her employer. "Because today's the day, that's why."

"Oh, no," said Jenna, closing her eyes. "Not today."

"Yes, today, and I can't believe you'd forget."

"Things have been a little...hectic, Liz, what with being arrested and all."

"Oh, that!" Liz dismissed the incident with a wave of her well-manicured hand. "Frank told me that it was nothing. Put it out of your mind. You have more important things to think about."

Jenna's dark brows knotted over the bridge of her nose. "I think I'll postpone it until next week."

"Don't postpone anything on my account," Chase said. Not that he knew what they were postponing.

"Mind your own business," Jenna snapped. "This has nothing to do with you."

"Jenna!" Liz stepped back. "If you don't want to go through with it, just say so."

Jenna considered the wisdom of kicking him in the shins but thought better of it. He'd probably find a way to further humiliate her. "Liz, I don't know what got into me." She placed a hand on the other woman's shoulder. "I'm sorry."

"You've been working really hard this past month," Liz said. "I know you haven't been yourself."

"That's it," said Jenna. "I haven't been myself at all."

"So that's your problem," said Chase.

She leaned over and aimed an elbow at his ribs.

"What are you doing?" Liz asked. "Does your arm hurt you?"

"Just stretching," Jenna said nonchalantly.

"Don't try that again," Chase warned, "unless you want to really have something to explain."

"You wouldn't dare," Jenna said.

"Of course I would," said Liz, oblivious to what was going on. "Mavis said if I didn't, she'd take back the wedding chapel."

"Mavis can't take back the chapel," Jenna said with a grin. "She already signed the controlling interest over to me."

"A promise is a promise," Liz said with mock seriousness. "And I promised Mavis I'd watch out for you."

"Who's Mavis?" Chase asked.

"We had lunch together last week," Jenna said to Liz. "She's happy as a lark out there on the lake and she didn't pester me once."

"She doesn't need to," Liz said sagely. "She has me to do it for her."

"Who's Mavis?" Chase repeated.

"Mind your own business!" Jenna immediately regretted the words when she saw the look on Liz's face.

"Jenna, a simple no would suffice." The woman looked as if she was about to burst into tears.

"Yes," said Jenna with a sigh. "I'll do it."

Chapter Seven

"What's so terrible about a blind date?" Jenna asked a few hours later as she touched up her lipstick. "You make it sound like I'm going to stand on a street corner and yell, 'Hey, sailor.'"

"You don't know anything about the guy," Chase said from the office sofa where he'd been sprawled out most of the morning. "I wouldn't go if I were you."

She snapped shut her compact and turned to meet his eyes. "That's what I was hoping you'd say." The thought of a blind date was horrible enough. A three-way blind date was horrendous. She started for the door. "I'll see you later."

He was next to her in a flash.

"Chase!" She stopped, hand on the doorknob. "Forget about it."

"This isn't my idea," he said. "Something jolted me off the sofa."

"A guilty conscience, maybe?"

"Why would I have a guilty conscience?"

"Because you're ruining my life, that's why."

"I'm not the one forcing you on a blind date."

"Liz didn't force me." She paused a moment. "I acquiesced."

"You caved."

"She thought I was insulting her. What was I supposed to do, hurt her feelings?"

"You didn't mind hurting *my* feelings."

"You don't *have* feelings."

"Forget it." He looked downright disgusted. "I have better things to do than tag along on a blind date with you and Dudley Do-Right."

She barely suppressed a laugh. "His name is Donald Doherty and he's an accountant in L.A."

"And he has to fly all the way to Las Vegas to find a date?" He shook his head. "The guy's a loser."

"Spoken by a man who's spent the last two years alone in a mine."

"At least I can find my own women."

"Finding and keeping are two different things."

"I never had any complaints."

"You never stayed around long enough to find out."

Oh, no, thought Jenna as she saw the open curiosity in his eyes. She should have quit while she was ahead.

"How would you know?" he asked.

"Lucky guess."

"The hell it is. Did we ever—"

"Good grief, no!"

"That's what I thought. I'd remember someone like you."

"Save the phony compliments for a more naive woman."

"You said you worked at the Paradise?"

She nodded.

"Can't figure why I never asked you out."

"Maybe I didn't want you to."

"That can't be it."

"Want to bet?" She raised a hand. "We've been through this already. We're not exactly a match made in heaven and, if you'll excuse me, I'm off to see if Donald and I are."

Head held high, she marched down the hallway. It would have looked great on the instant replay except for the fact that Chase marched right alongside her.

"You're not coming with us," she murmured as they neared the main lobby.

"Can't help it," he murmured back. "'Whither thou goest' and all of that."

Liz was waiting for her near the reception desk. "You didn't change your clothes."

"This is fine for a lunch date, Liz."

Liz wrinkled her nose. "I suppose so, but if I had your body I'd probably be showing a lot more skin."

"Skin," said Chase. "Sounds good to me."

"So where's my date?" asked Jenna.

"Freshening up," said Liz.

"Women freshen up," said Chase. "Men use the john."

"Oh, shut up."

"Really, Jenna!" Liz's voice rose in irritation. "I thought we were friends."

"I wasn't talking to you," Jenna said.

Liz's eyebrows rose practically to her hairline. "Then who *were* you talking to, your guardian angel?"

"Let's see you get out of this one," Chase said.

"My stomach," said Jenna. "It's been growling all morning. I finally had to tell it to shut up."

"Good save," said Chase. "Let's see if she buys it."

God bless Liz. She did buy it. Jenna made a mental note to give the woman a raise for service above and beyond the call of duty... or friendship.

"There he is," Liz said in a breathless voice. "Isn't he a hunk?"

"He's very attractive," Jenna admitted as the man strode toward them.

"You think he's good-looking?" Chase asked. "The guy's bowlegged."

"Donald plays polo on the weekends," Liz went on.

"Horses," said Chase. "That'll do it every time."

"A polo-playing accountant?" Jenna asked. "Isn't that a pricey sport?"

Donald Doherty stopped right in front of Jenna and flashed her a smile that would do his Beverly Hills dentist proud. "Blind dates were never like this when I was in high school."

"Did you hear that line?" Chase groaned. "Bet he does great in accounting circles."

She ignored Chase and extended her hand toward Donald. "I'm Jenna Grey."

Her date enfolded her hand in his two and held on. "Donald Doherty." His smile widened. "My friends call me Donny."

"How long is he going to hang onto your hand?" Chase griped. "You'd think it was a religious experience."

Jenna, who had been wondering the same thing, gently reclaimed her hand.

"You two make a beautiful couple," Liz said. She sounded like the mother of the bride. "I'm so glad you flew in for the day, Donald."

"You flew in just for lunch?" Jenna asked, flattered despite herself.

"Good women are hard to find," Donald said, still smiling. "What's a one-hour plane flight in the face of that?"

"The guy's desperate," Chase said.

"I made reservations for lunch at the Paradise Hotel," Donald said.

"The Venetian Room?" Jenna asked.

"Probably the buffet," said Chase.

She couldn't help it. She kicked Chase squarely in the shin.

"Are you a dancer?" Donald asked. "That was a pretty neat step."

"Why don't you kick *him?*" Chase asked. "He's the one with the bad tie."

"I like the tie."

Donald looked a tad puzzled. He fingered his tie and turned toward Liz, who beamed with almost maternal pride.

"That's wonderful!" Liz clasped her hands and looked from Jenna to Donald. "Ties are such a personal thing."

Donald put his hand beneath Jenna's elbow. "I'll tell you where I buy them," he said as they started for the door.

"This is going to be some afternoon," Chase grumbled as they walked toward the white stretch limo idling at the curb. "Maybe we can all go shopping."

Jenna had to bite her tongue to keep from blurting out another sharp retort. *Go away,* she thought, aiming a blistering look in Chase's direction. How was she supposed to remember that he was invisible to the rest of the world when he was standing there next to poor Donald, making the L.A. accountant fade into the woodwork? She didn't imagine there were many men on the planet who could hold their own against Chase Quinn. When they were giving out sex appeal, he'd obviously come back for seconds.

The limo driver opened the door for them. Jenna hesitated a moment, and Chase used the opportunity to climb right in and make himself comfortable on the seat adjacent to the television and stereo system.

"No choice in the matter," he said with a self-satisfied grin. "The curse made me do it."

Jenna settled herself in the rear seat. Donald settled himself right next to her.

"We have table number one," Donald said as the driver moved out into traffic. "I hear it's the best."

"How wonderful," Jenna said. She'd always wanted to dine at the Venetian Room but somehow she'd imagined herself with someone more dynamic than the affable Mr. Doherty. *Someone like Chase, maybe?* She tried to focus on the man sitting next to her but it was the man across from her who commanded her attention.

She and Donald made pleasant small talk as they rode to the Paradise Hotel, and she prayed he had no idea how bored she was. It wasn't Donald's fault. Under normal circumstances he was probably a thoroughly swell fellow. It was simply his misfortune to come into her life at the same time as Chase.

Not that she was interested in Chase Quinn. A woman would have to be out of her mind to take him seriously. The man was born to the hunt. She knew the type well. The name of the game was conquest, and once that conquest was assured, he moved on.

Too bad she also knew how exciting it would be while it lasted.

"Don't you think so?" Donald asked.

She blinked, trying to remember what on earth they'd been talking about. "Oh, yes," she bluffed. "Absolutely."

"He was talking about flying saucers," Chase offered. "He thinks they landed in the San Fernando Valley during the last earthquake."

Donald launched into an animated discourse on the inevitability of alien visitors and how hard it was to find a woman who understood how important it was to greet those aliens warmly. Jenna was wondering what on earth Liz had been thinking when she put the two of them together when Chase reached for the champagne in the bar and began to ease the cork from the bottle.

"Cheers!" He tipped the champagne toward his mouth.

"Might as well take advantage of the bar," Donald said, choosing that moment to work up a thirst. "It's all on the old expense account."

"No!"

Donald stared at her as if she'd grown a second head.

Chase paused, bottle at his lips.

"Hey," said Donald, "if you don't want a drink just say so."

"I don't want a drink," she said, praying Chase would put the bottle down before Donald turned around.

"Do you mind if I have one?"

"No—I mean, yes. Actually I do."

Donald's smile dimmed a few watts. "Liz didn't tell me you were a teetotaler."

"I'm not," she said as Chase took another pull on the bottle.

"So there's no problem if I help myself."

"We're almost at the Paradise," she stammered. "Maybe—"

Too late. Donald turned toward the bar just in time to see the bottle of Mumm's drifting into position.

"Did you see that?" His voice trembled with disbelief.

Jenna took a deep breath and went for broke. "See what?"

"The bottle. It . . . flew."

"Donald," she said, wishing she was any place but there, "bottles don't fly."

"You must've seen it," Donald insisted. "The damn bottle flew about two, three feet."

You poor man. I hope your next blind date is a better woman than I am. "Were you drinking before you picked me up, Donald?"

"I had a Bloody Mary on the plane, but that's not enough—" He stopped and looked at her closely. "You really didn't see it?"

She shook her head and kept her crossed fingers out of sight. "I really didn't see it."

"You're covering for me," Chase said. "I like that in a wife."

"I'm not going to be your wife!" *Now you did it, Jenna.*

Donald looked as if he'd been sucker punched. His nervous laughter bounced around them. "Listen, I don't know what Liz told you, but I'm not looking to get into anything serious. Not that I have anything against marriage—hey, I'm as much a family man as the next guy—but I'm still building my nest egg and . . ."

"HE'S NOT COMING BACK," Chase said as they waited in the lobby of the Paradise Hotel behind the suspended shark tank with the treasure chest filled with doubloons.

"He's coming back," Jenna said. "It's part of the curse."

"You used the M word. Trust me, he's not coming back."

"I didn't propose to him, for heaven's sake. I said I *wasn't* going to get married."

"Doesn't matter," Chase said, thoroughly enjoying himself. "You mentioned marriage. That's enough to send most red-blooded men riding off into the sunset."

"Men are weird," she said, watching the steady stream of visitors strolling past, wondering if a certain accountant from L.A. would be among them. "Marriage is the natural order of things."

"Glad to hear you say that."

She met his eyes. "That doesn't mean I want to marry *you.*"

He made a show of glancing around. "I don't see anyone else knocking on your door."

"I'll have you know plenty of men have knocked on my door."

He lifted her left hand and checked her ring finger, as he had once before. "Still no wedding ring."

She pulled her hand back and plunged it into the pocket of her trousers.

"Broke a lot of hearts?" he asked.

"Haven't you heard?" she countered. "I don't break hearts, I put them back together again."

He felt as if she'd landed a blow right in the center of his chest. There'd been other men. For a lot of reasons, he didn't want to think about it. Beneath the fire and the flash, there was a real woman, and that real woman had a very breakable heart.

Strange it hadn't occurred to him before. He'd been so taken by her beauty and quick wit—and so obsessed with his unique situation—that he hadn't given a hell of a lot of thought to the fact that she also had feelings and that those feelings ran deep.

"Come on," he said. "Your bean counter's halfway to Rodeo Drive by now. Why don't we grab some lunch?"

She opened her mouth to answer, but an elderly couple stopped next to her to adjust the laces on the woman's running shoes. It was hard enough to remember that Chase was invisible to everyone but her. The last thing she wanted was to propel this innocent couple into cardiac arrest.

"You're not hungry?" he asked. "I wouldn't mind strolling around, checking out the action in the casino."

She opened her eyes as wide as she could and inclined her head toward the man and woman next to her.

"What?" he asked. "You want to ask them to come along?"

She shook her head and pointed at the couple with her right thumb. *Don't be obtuse, Quinn. You know what I'm trying to tell you.*

"They don't gamble? They're not hungry?"

Her right hand clenched into a fist.

"You're gonna hit me again," he said, raising his hands and stepping backward in mock surrender. "Have you ever thought about going into boxing?"

The elderly man and woman drifted into the crowd.

"You idiot!" Jenna exploded. "Did you want to scare those poor people half to death?"

"You wouldn't have scared them," Chase said, all male logic and reason. "They'd just have thought you were crazy."

"Thanks a lot." To her amazement she started to smile. "Although I've begun to wonder the same thing myself."

"You're not crazy," he said.

Her smile widened. "You don't know me well enough to say that."

"The situation's crazy," he said. "You're as sane as they come."

She blinked in surprise. "Do you realize that's the first nice thing you've said to me?"

"Don't let it go to your head." His answering smile softened the words.

"Amazing," she said with a gentle shake of her head. "Life is absolutely amazing. I can't get rid of you and I can't hang on to anybody else."

"Why would you want to?"

She knew what he meant but couldn't help herself. "Hang on to someone?"

"Get rid of me."

"It's what you want, isn't it?"

Up until that moment he'd thought it was.

They considered each other as the noise and activity around them seemed to fade away. He noted the vulnerability beneath the deep intelligence. She felt the pain beneath the bravado.

"Chase?" Her tone was curious. So was the look in her eyes. "It *is* what you want."

"Damn right," he said, as the world came back into focus.

"They have a great buffet here," she said, trying to pretend she didn't feel the pull of something as frightening as it was wonderful. "Not that a headliner like you probably spent a lot of time waiting for the peel-it-yourself shrimp cocktail." A hotel employee looked at her strangely, and she couldn't blame him. Talking to yourself wasn't socially acceptable, not even in Las Vegas. "I'll fill a plate for us if you promise not to dance on the tabletops."

"I can manage that," he said. An unfamiliar sensation was spreading outward from the center of his chest, making him aware of the rhythmic beat of his heart, the tempo of his breathing, the way he wanted her to keep smiling like that just a little bit longer.

JENNA WASN'T SMILING two hours later when the cab delivered them to the rear entrance of Fantasy Weddings.

"You idiot!" she said through clenched teeth. "Of all the ridiculous stunts to pull, that takes the cake."

"You wanted some more chicken salad. I got it for you. What's the big deal?"

"What's the big deal?" she parroted as the cab drove away. "They had to perform CPR on the man sitting next to us."

"But I got you the last of the chicken salad—"

"Chase!" Her voice rose in frustration. "I know people at the Paradise. I don't want them to think I'm crazy."

"They don't think you're crazy. They offered you a job, didn't they?"

"As a magician!" What else would explain a floating dinner plate piled high with chicken salad?

"You're quick," he said. "I was impressed."

"I've run out of excuses," she said, reaching for the door. "This can't go on."

Her heels clicked down the hallway. The rap of Chase's boots followed close behind.

"Marry me," he said as she picked up speed, "and this will all be a distant memory."

"Be quiet before—"

"Jenna!" Grace popped out of the ladies' room. "I thought I heard you. Thank God you're here. We have a problem."

"The air-conditioning," she said, mentally calculating how many couples they'd have to marry to pay for repairs. "I was afraid it wouldn't be enough."

"Not the air-conditioning." Grace's tone was clipped. "It's Gil."

Jenna understood what it meant to have your blood run cold. "Has he hurt Rosalia?"

"He's looking for her."

"Yes!" Jenna pumped the air with her fist. "She left him."

Grace didn't seem to share Jenna's enthusiasm.

"What's wrong?" Jenna asked. "Don't tell me you think she should stay with the bastard?"

Grace lowered her voice. "He's in your office."

"He has no business being in my office, Grace."

Grace flushed. "He's been drinking. We—we decided it would be safer with him out of the way."

"Damn fool," Chase growled. "She should've called the cops and had him hauled away."

Jenna tended to agree with him but for once she remembered to keep her mouth shut. "I'll take care of Gil," she said in a determined voice. Wheeling, she headed down the hallway to her office.

"The guy's no good," Chase said. "Let me handle it."

"This is my business, he's my problem. You stay out of it."

"The guy's dangerous."

"I'm not Rosalia. He won't lay a hand on me."

"A bastard's a bastard. If he blows up, he'll hit whoever's closest."

"Stay out of it," she warned. "I don't need you to fight my battles for me."

He started to say he wasn't looking to fight her battles, that he hated bullies and wanted to grab the opportunity to knock one on his butt, but he decided against it. What difference did it make, anyway? Like she said, it was her problem. He'd just hang around and make sure the guy didn't get out of line.

The door to her office was open. Gil stood near the window, nursing a bottle of beer. She felt the adrenaline rush from head to foot as he turned to face her.

"Where is she?" Gil demanded.

Jenna glided into the room. "Rosalia hasn't been in to work for two days."

"You didn't answer my question," he said as Jenna took her seat behind the desk. "Where is she?"

Chase stood a foot away from Gil, arms folded tightly across his chest.

"I don't know where she is," Jenna said, flipping through the messages next to the telephone. "All I know is we need her here at work, and I hope she shows up soon."

Gil approached her, with Chase close behind him. "You don't like me."

"You're right," Jenna said, meeting his eyes head on. "I don't."

He leaned across the desk. Dark stubble peppered his jaw. A gold cap glittered from his left upper incisor. "We didn't have none of these problems until you came along, filling her head with crap about the way it's supposed to be with us." He clutched the bottle of beer in his right hand, the hand he had right under Jenna's nose. She hated the flat yeasty smell of beer, and it took all her self-control to keep from slapping that hand away. "Keep away from us, lady, or you'll be sorry."

She reached for the telephone with a display of calm that didn't match the turmoil inside her chest. "This is Jenna Grey at Fantasy Weddings. We have an intruder here who—"

Gil yanked the wire from the jack. The phone skidded across her desk and crashed to the floor near Chase's feet. She flinched at the noise, but Chase acted as if nothing had happened. She waited for him to grab Gil or block him or land a punch against the guy's jaw, but he continued to stand there, watching the proceedings with almost impassive curiosity.

Isn't that what you wanted, Jenna? You told him to stay out of your business.

But somehow she'd never expected him to do it.

Gil's rage was palpable. "Mess with me, lady, and it's the last thing you'll do."

She rose from her chair. "Are you threatening me?"

"Take it any way you want. Just don't try to come between me and Rosa." With that Gil stormed from the office. Seconds later the back door slammed shut behind him.

"Good riddance," Jenna said, trying to pretend she wasn't shaking like a leaf in a strong wind. "I hope Rosalia never goes back to him."

"You've got guts, lady," Chase said. "You're crazy but you've got guts."

She didn't say anything. Truth was, she felt oddly disappointed, as if he'd broken a promise or somehow let her down, even though he had done exactly what she'd asked him to do—nothing.

"Are you okay?" Grace appeared in the open doorway not six inches from Chase. "I called the police from the phone in my office."

"Call and tell them everything's fine," Jenna said, trying to shake off the melancholy mood that was settling itself across her shoulders. "Gil won't be back."

Grace frowned then sniffed the air. "Wood smoke and spice," she said. "You wouldn't think a lowlife like him would wear such a classy after-shave."

"Thanks," said Chase, his wicked grin reappearing, "but that's my classy after-shave you're sniffing."

"Waste of a great cologne," said Grace with a sigh.

Chase aimed a look at Jenna but she didn't respond. This whole bizarre thing with the mine and the curse and the invisible man had been fun in a crazy kind of way, but it wasn't fun any longer. She wanted it over, the whole thing, wanted him out of her life before she fell any more deeply—

"The police," Jenna said, pushing away the strange thoughts. A headache had blossomed behind her right eye, and all she wanted was to be alone. "You'd better call them now."

"Right," said Grace. She turned to leave then stopped. "How could I forget? We got a call from Lido Tours. A wide-body jet from Tokyo will be arriving at McCarran in an hour, and half the passengers are engaged couples looking to tie the knot in the good ol' U.S. of A. The way things are going Fantasy Weddings'll break even before the first week is out.''

Jenna looked at Chase, who had dropped to his right knee in a parody of a romantic proposal.

If I live that long, she thought.

Chapter Eight

The afternoon went downhill from there.

Half of the couples from Tokyo spoke no English, and Jenna had to scramble to find a minister with enough command of the Japanese language to perform forty ceremonies in their native tongue.

Then there was the expected problem with the air-conditioning, the unexpected malfunction in the men's room, and the fact that Jenna slowly but surely was coming to grips with the fact that there was no way out of the mess her life had become.

At one point after the Japanese weddings, she'd started to ask Chase a question about the mine when he vanished right before her eyes, and a sense of panic rose up in Jenna that was completely out of proportion to the situation. He'd disappeared on her before, but she'd always been able to hear him, catch the scent of wood smoke and spice in the air. But this time it was as if he'd never existed.

Then, just as a cry rose up to fill her throat, he was back in front of her.

"What happened?" She touched his forearm, as if to reassure herself of his existence.

"You missed me," he had said, grinning. "Somehow I didn't think you would."

He'd deflected every question with a joke or a wisecrack, and her sense of unease heightened exponentially as the evening wore on.

But it did serve to point out one very important truth. She had to put an end to this situation before she lost her mind. And there was a way out. That's what he'd been trying to tell her, but she refused to listen.

Marriage.

The one thing she'd always wanted, and now it was turning into a travesty.

All she'd ever wanted was a home and a family. Was that asking so darned much of life? Was there a secret handshake she didn't know about, a password that moved on from mother to daughter that no one had passed on to her? There had to be some reason that millions of other women had husbands and children, and she had no one at all.

Across the room, Chase shifted position and flung an arm out to the side, toppling a vase of flowers from the walnut coffee table. She watched as a puddle of water spread across the floor, lapping gently against the table's chunky legs.

Mr. Right could walk into her life tomorrow and there wouldn't be a single thing she could do about it and all because of the man asleep on her sofa.

She crumpled up a piece of notepaper and tossed it in his direction. It fell short and settled into the pool of water. She crumpled up another one, aimed, then fired. It brushed against his arm and he grumbled in his sleep and pulled his arm against his chest. Encouraged by her skill, she grabbed several sheets of paper, crunched them into a ball roughly the size of an orange, then lobbed it toward him.

Perfect shot. Right between those golden eyes.

"What the hell—?" He sat up, resting on one elbow, rumpled, cranky, too damn sexy for his own good. Or for hers. He focused on her. "Using me for target practice?" He barely stifled a yawn.

"Could be."

He swung his feet to the floor and dragged his fingers through his hair. "You're not good at the subtle approach. If you've got something to say, say it."

"You're ruining my life."

"That's good for a start."

"I want you to go away."

"Even better."

"And I'll marry you."

The look on his face was so comical that she laughed despite herself.

"What was that?" he demanded.

"I said I'll marry you. I don't want to but I can't think of another way out."

"A ringing declaration of love from the blushing bride."

"Love has nothing to do with any of this," she said brusquely. "You should know that better than anyone."

The end was finally near. He waited for the rush of exhilaration to come, but all he felt was an emptiness so deep inside it seemed part of his bones. He was only a pair of *I do*s away from reclaiming his life, yet all he could think of was the sad look in her beautiful eyes.

You're getting soft, Quinn, he told himself. *Don't waste time daydreaming. Take those vows and get it over with.*

"Las Vegas makes it easy to get married," she was saying.

"How easy is it to get divorced?"

Her look was sharp. "Believe me, that won't be a problem."

"So let's do it." He stood up. "Let's get the show on the road."

"THEY'RE A SUSPICIOUS GROUP," Chase said as they headed out of town in Jenna's Volkswagen an hour later. "They act more like your family than your employees."

"They like to worry." Jenna checked her side mirror then changed lanes. "You have to admit I've given them plenty of reason the last two days." Fantasy Weddings had finally opened, and she was spending more time out of the office than in. Definitely not the highway to success.

"This time tomorrow everything will be back to normal."

"I don't think I remember what normal was."

Neither did he. It occurred to Chase that once the curse was broken he faced the task of reclaiming a life that had been suspended without warning almost two years ago. Walking around the Paradise with Jenna that afternoon, he'd learned a few things he would've been happier not knowing. The powers that be hadn't wasted any time booking his replacement, and no matter how hard he looked he couldn't find any evidence that for a while he'd been the biggest draw on the Strip.

"It's almost ten o'clock," Chase said. "How do you know your friend Mavis will still be up?"

"She'll be up." Jenna kept her eyes focused on the highway ahead. "Mavis is a night owl." If Mavis wasn't up, Jenna would stand there and ring the doorbell until the entire neighborhood was up.

"What if she won't marry us?"

"Don't worry. She'll marry us." Mavis had spent forty years of her life marrying couples who had no business getting together in the first place. Jenna and Chase would be the icing on the cake. "I'll even pay the twenty-eight dollars for the license."

"The bride is eager."

"The bride is desperate. I'd go over Hoover Dam in a barrel if it meant you'd go away and leave me alone."

"I'll be gone as soon as we say 'I do.'"

"I'll hold you to that."

"Trust me, lady, this isn't my idea of a marriage made in heaven."

Grim-faced, she pressed the pedal to the metal.

"How're you going to explain me?" he asked a few miles later.

"I don't know." She hadn't even thought of that. The man was invisible. Mavis would think she'd lost her mind. But then why should Mavis be any different?

"You'd better think of something."

"You think of something," she shot back. "You're the one with the problem."

"She's your friend."

"I'm not invisible, you're the one who—" She let out a loud, exasperated sigh. They were beginning to sound like spoiled six-year-olds fighting over playground space. Six-year-olds with sexual tension up the wazoo. "What I'd like to know is what I did to deserve this. I never break the speed limit. I recycle. I pay my taxes on time. Why am I being punished?"

"Bad attitude, Jenna."

"Is it any wonder? I didn't ask for this. Maybe if you'd stayed out of that damned mine like any sane person, none of this would have happened."

"No guts, no glory."

"No brain, no gain."

"Right, princess," he said in a tone she hadn't heard before. "You've had everything handed to you your whole life. What would you know about taking chances?"

Her fingers curved more tightly around the wheel. Sometimes it seemed to Jenna as if she'd spent her whole life taking chances, praying that one day she'd hit the jackpot and find happiness.

He watched her with unblinking curiosity, and she wondered if he could see through her defenses. She hoped he couldn't. They were all she had.

"You don't know anything about me, Quinn," she said evenly. "I'd just as soon keep it that way."

But he did know something about her, something she wished she could erase from his memory bank forever. He knew that she wanted him more than she'd wanted any other man, and the proof of that was the glorious life-size statue of him she'd fashioned from loneliness and desire.

MAVIS SUMMER had retired eighteen months ago to a luxurious house by a golf course near Lake Mead. Mavis liked to say she was too old for the bright lights and fast pace of Las Vegas, but Jenna knew the truth. John Olin lived in the same upscale development, and if Mavis had her way, they'd be merging their retirement accounts before too long.

Jenna was a wreck by the time she parked her VW in the driveway next to Mavis's bright red sports car. How on earth was she going to explain the mess her life had become? *Surprise, Mavis! This is Chase, my intended. Remember what you said about us being perfect for each other? Well, yes he's invisible, but there's no law against that, is there?*

"What're you going to tell her?" Chase asked as they walked up to the front door. "She's bound to have a few questions."

"I might plead temporary insanity and throw myself on her mercy."

"Just make sure she marries us before she has you locked up."

"Your concern warms my heart."

He started to say something, but she quelled him with a glance. Gathering her resolve, she rang the doorbell.

"I'm comin', I'm comin'." Mavis's voice, vibrant and distinct, sounded from inside the sprawling Spanish style house. "You better have a good reason for botherin' me at this hour."

Chase looked at Jenna. "I thought you said she was a night owl."

Jenna considered making a run for it. "She is...at least she always used to be." In the old days eleven o'clock was the beginning of the evening.

"Maybe you should've called."

"I wasn't thinking about good manners," she snapped. "I was thinking about getting rid of you, you—"

"Jenna!" The door swung open and Mavis, barely five feet tall on tiptoe, grabbed Jenna in a huge bear hug. "Sakes alive, am I getting old? I thought you were coming for dinner on—" She stopped mid-sentence. Her brown eyes widened, then Jenna watched in amazement as a smile of delight creased the older woman's perpetually tanned face. "Chase Quinn, as I live and breathe. I was just thinking about you last night!"

Jenna didn't mean to faint. She wasn't the kind of woman given to swooning or the vapors, but this was the last straw. Her ears buzzed, the world swam out of focus, and she felt herself going under.

"Doesn't eat enough," she heard Mavis say as the world rushed back to meet her moments later. "Girl that tall needs some fuel to get through the day."

She pushed herself up on one elbow and discovered she was lying on the hot pink sofa in Mavis's living room. Mavis was perched on the arm, a vision in a fluorescent purple nightgown decorated with matching marabou feathers. Chase was crouched down next to Jenna, and for a moment she thought she saw genuine concern in his golden eyes. But only for a moment. She knew his only true concern was saving his own hide.

"You can see him," she said to Mavis.

"Of course I can see him," Mavis retorted. "I might be old but, thank the good Lord, I still have my eyesight."

"That's not what I mean, Mavis."

Mavis turned toward Chase. "You sit here with her, boy. I'm going to call the doctor." She touched her forefinger to her temple in an unmistakable gesture. "I think she might've hit her head."

"I didn't hit my head." Jenna sat up, shaky but unbowed. "He's invisible. I'm the only one who can see him." She turned to Chase. "Right?"

Mavis's brown eyes filled with tears. "Oh, Lordy," she said low. "My poor girl's done it this time." She headed for the phone. "Too much hard work. That's what did it."

"Do something!" Jenna ordered Chase. "You know I'm not crazy. Tell her!"

Chase rose to his feet and intercepted Mavis a few feet away from the bright pink telephone. "She's right, Mavis. Her head is fine. I *am* invisible to everyone but you and Jenna."

Bless Mavis's adventurous heart. She didn't bat a false-lashed eye. "It's probably all tangled up with that curse on the old Tucker Mine."

"Mavis," said Jenna carefully, "you believe Chase is invisible?"

"No reason not to, child. If you say it and he believes it, that's proof enough for me."

"So then you know why we've come here?"

"Don't have a clue about that," Mavis said cheerfully, "but I figure you'll tell me in your own time."

"We have to get married," Jenna blurted then instantly regretted her choice of words when she saw the look of utter delight on Mavis's round face. "No, no," she quickly amended, "not like that. I mean—"

"It's the curse," Chase said, looking more gorgeous than an invisible man had any right to look.

Mavis nodded. "'What you most fear is what you must face.' A clever curse, that one, but sneaky as a ferret with an empty stomach."

"Marriage," said Chase.

Mavis's gaze sharpened. "Are you sure?" she asked Chase. "Seems to me that's a mighty simple solution to a mighty big problem."

"What else could it be?" Chase shot back.

"Lots of men spend their lives wriggling away from matrimony like a fish from a baited hook, but it isn't the institution that scares the bejesus out of 'em. It's love."

"Mavis." Jenna wasn't in the mood for either philosophy or intensive therapy. "He knows what he's afraid of better than you do and it's marriage. Case closed."

Mavis turned her attention to Jenna, who now wondered if she should have kept her mouth shut. "And you're willin' to be bride for a day."

"I don't have a choice."

"We always have choices."

"Not in this. I can't get rid of him unless I marry him."

"So you're the conduit. What did you do to bring him to you?"

"The statue," they said in unison.

"Ah." Mavis nodded sagely. "Sooner or later it all comes round to sex."

"Mavis," said Jenna, appalled. "You're making me wish I'd never come here."

"I know a thing or two about curses and spells, and the one thing that's always true is that the answer lies deep inside." She placed a hand on her plump bosom. "When you made that statue, you called him back into the world and now you're responsible for his fate."

"So where does the sex come in?" Chase asked.

"It doesn't," Jenna snapped. Leave it to him to bring the conversation back to the glandular.

His golden eyes glittered with amusement. "Can't blame me for asking."

"Chemistry," Mavis observed, nodding her head. "That's always a good start for a marriage."

"And a good ending," Jenna said. "I need a wedding, Mavis, but I don't want a marriage."

"Young people." Mavis sighed. "You always think you're the only ones who know what's going on, but I can tell you it takes an old person to give things perspective." She reached down, brushed a speck of dust from her bright purple mules then turned toward Chase. "You been married before?"

"Not me."

She winked at Jenna. "Don't have to ask you that, do I, honey?"

"That's right," Chase said, all innocence. "What was that story again?"

Mavis took the bait. "Three times left standing at the altar," the woman said before Jenna could open her mouth. "Not that it was any fault of her own. Jenna has a heart of gold, but when it comes to men she has the worst luck in the world."

Chase aimed a wicked grin at Jenna. "Looks like your luck has changed."

"Not so I've noticed."

"I'm not going anywhere."

"More's the pity."

"Maybe the fourth time's the charm."

It certainly didn't feel that way to Jenna.

"This had better work," she said as Mavis went to call John Olin to serve as one of the witnesses.

"I'm counting the minutes until I've seen the last of you."

"Why wouldn't it work? She marries us. The curse is broken. We divorce. It doesn't get simpler than that."

He had a point. "I'll call Frank in the morning. He can file the papers."

"Sounds good," said Chase. "Maybe he can help me find a place to live while he's at it."

"Frank's an attorney, not a real estate agent."

Mavis bustled into the room, carrying a vase filled with daisies and carnations. "John was mighty surprised but he said he'd be glad to come by and lend a hand. He's calling that uppity neighbor of his, the widow lady with the French poodle, to be the other witness." Mavis's lips thinned to a narrow line of displeasure. "Gray hair," she said with a shake of her own bright yellow curls. "You'd think she'd never heard of hair dye before."

Chase, who had been watching Mavis with astonished admiration, threw back his head and laughed loud and long. "Damn good thing I'm spoken for, Mavis, or I'd be giving John a run for his money."

Mavis dimpled at him. "Lot of sweet talk," she said, obviously pleased. "I'm afraid I'd be too much woman for you."

Chase drew Mavis into a lighthearted conversation, and Jenna found herself silently listening to the two of them. She'd never imagined he could be so warm and open and downright amusing. There was no mocking edge to him as he talked to Mavis, no insincerity. He genuinely liked the older woman as much as she liked him, and Jenna experienced a sharp nip of jealousy.

Mavis is eighty-two years old, you idiot! Besides, even if Mavis was twenty-two, it didn't matter. There was nothing between herself and Chase Quinn that marriage and divorce wouldn't cure.

"ARE YOU SURE this is legal?" Jenna asked as she and Chase took their places behind the Chinese silk trifold screen in Mavis's living room. "Don't the witnesses have to see us get married?"

"Remember the skydivers?" Mavis replied. "Only the preacher jumped with them. The witnesses stayed on the ground."

"She sounds pretty, Mavis," John called from the foyer. "Bet she's a redhead. I always did have me a yen for redheads."

Gloria, the widow lady with the French poodle, giggled. "I used to be a redhead, Johnny."

"Damn fool," Mavis muttered. "She'd better keep her mitts off my man."

"Let's get started," Chase said. "The quicker we do it, the quicker this mess is over and done with."

"Don't blame you, sonny," John called out. "A groom should be eager on his wedding night."

"Are you naked back there?" Gloria chirped. "My best friend was a nudist and she got married underwater so they wouldn't scare her mother-in-law."

"I'm hallucinating," Jenna said. "This can't be happening to me."

But it was, and five minutes later, to the amazement of all concerned, she and Chase were husband and wife.

Chapter Nine

"What are you waitin' for?" Mavis asked as she flipped shut the Book of Common Prayer. "Kiss your bride, boy!"

"You heard her," Chase said as he drew an unwilling Jenna into his arms. "It's not legal if we don't kiss."

She tried to put a good face on it for their audience, but it was obvious his brand-new wife was feeling anything but romantic.

"Notice anything different?" she said through tightly clenched teeth as he dipped his mouth to meet hers.

"You kissed a lot better last night."

He felt the not-so-subtle pressure of her dainty shoe atop his instep. "You know what I'm talking about. Are you still invisible?"

"You tell me," he said, his lips against hers. "Can you see me?"

"I want to know if *they* can see you."

"What's going on back there?" John called out. "Can't wait to start the honeymoon?"

Chase took Jenna's hand. "Let's see where we stand."

Mavis pulled the screen aside.

John and Gloria and Gloria's poodle flocked to Jenna's side.

"Where's the lucky groom?" Gloria cried.

"Over here." Chase stepped in front of the woman.

She ignored him.

"I wanted to shake his hand, but at least let me kiss the bride." The old guy made to plant one on Jenna's cheek but plowed right into Chase's left biceps instead and lost his balance.

Jenna reached out to steady him. John recovered and kissed her soundly.

"I may need to get my bifocals checked, but I can still recognize a pretty woman when I see one and you are one beautiful lady." He glanced around the room. "So where did your new hubby go?"

"The excitement got to the boy," said Mavis with a wink for Chase. "He's in the loo."

"Poor darling," cooed Gloria, batting her eyes in John's direction. "Some men are so afraid of marriage." She patted John's arm. "Isn't that the silliest thing?"

Mavis was nobody's fool, and she placed a proprietary hand on John's arm. "It sure is silly," she said. "John and I were talkin' about that just the other night, weren't we?"

Conversation flowed around, over and straight through Chase while he stood there, wondering what the hell had gone wrong.

He grabbed Jenna's hand again. "We're getting out of here."

Jenna lurched toward the door.

"Aren't you going to wait for your hubby?" John called out.

"Somehow I know he'll catch up with her, John." Mavis, who was thoroughly enjoying the spectacle, laughed and waved goodbye.

Once outside Jenna broke away from her new husband and stormed toward her car.

"This is your fault." She opened the door of her VW. "Everything is your fault."

"I married you, didn't I? That's more than the three guys before me managed to do."

"You're lucky I don't throw that statue of you into Lake Mead and be done with the whole thing."

"Go ahead. The bottom of Lake Mead's got to be warmer than sitting next to you."

She started the engine on the second try. "I'm calling Frank as soon as I get home," she said as the car lurched down the driveway.

"What for?"

"An annulment."

"You can't get an annulment."

"Why not?" She headed for the highway to Las Vegas. "It's obvious the wedding didn't work. You're still invisible."

"You're rushing things. Maybe it takes time to break a curse."

"Maybe you weren't as afraid of marriage as you thought."

"Believe me, I'm making up for that now."

"This hasn't been exactly a picnic for me, either, Quinn."

He couldn't put his finger on exactly what it was or why it happened. Was it that odd note of sadness, that hint of regret in her voice? Even he knew that brief ceremony in Mavis's house wasn't the stuff of dreams. Whatever it was, he felt the movement inside his chest, the slipping forward of his heart in that same slow dance of tectonic plates shifting into newer and more dangerous patterns.

Had she loved any of those men? Or had she just wanted someone to love her? He watched as the moon dappled her face with silvery light and tried to imagine Jenna Grey in love. He'd seen her confused, he'd seen her surprised by desire. But in love? No matter how hard he tried, he couldn't bring the image to life.

A FEW MILES before the city limits, Jenna swung off the highway and onto an unpaved road headed east.

"I don't know why I didn't think of this before," she said as much to herself as to Chase. "The answer is so simple that it's laughable."

He peered out the window into the darkness until a familiar landmark jogged his memory. "The mine," he said, turning to look at her. "Why?"

"You heard Mavis. There's an inherent logic to curses, even the most outlandish of them. We did everything we were supposed to do. Now the only thing that's missing is closure."

"Are you saying we go into the mine?"

It was obvious that thought didn't thrill her. "I don't know what I'm saying. All I know is that we have to do something."

Chase had to admit there was a certain symmetry to her plan that appealed to him. It reminded him of the rituals of magic, the bracketing of an extraordinary event with details so ordinary they went unnoticed. He leaned forward, peering out the window into the darkness.

"The road branches about a half mile up. Bear left and the mine's two hundred yards straight ahead."

"So much for my bright idea," Jenna said as she brought the car to a stop near the entrance to the mine. "They've boarded it up."

Wooden planks had been nailed across the opening, and a huge danger sign was posted.

"I wonder what they're afraid of," Chase said.

"There was a big uproar when you disappeared. Some people said it was the curse that took you, others said the mine was unsafe and you'd been lost in a collapse somewhere deep inside."

"Now what?" he asked.

"I don't know," said Jenna.

They fell silent. The only noise was the rustle of the wind across the desert. He waited to hear a voice or see a vision, something that would tell him he'd reached the end of the long road back.

"I don't think this is working," she said.

"Why should this be any different? So far nothing's worked."

"And you said *I* had a bad attitude. At least I'm trying to come up with a solution."

"Right," he said. "Sitting in front of the mine in a beat-up VW is a great solution."

"I haven't heard you come up with anything better."

"I think you were right the first time."

"About what?" *Please don't say you want to go into the mine.*

Of course that was exactly what he did say. "What's the worst thing that can happen, they double curse me? You can't be any more invisible than I already am."

"Call me crazy, but I don't want to become the world's first invisible woman."

He met her eyes in the moonlight, and his breath caught. "That would be a waste."

She'd been deflecting comments like that since puberty. She knew how little they meant in the scheme of things, yet there was something about his words—or maybe the way he said them—that kindled a spark deep inside.

"I'm your wife," she tossed back. "Save your flattery for your girlfriend."

"I'm a one-woman man. There is no girl-friend."

"A temporary situation, I'm sure. The minute the curse is broken you'll be back to your old tricks."

"And you know all about my old tricks."

"Show girls have a lot of time between perform-ances," she said, "and they spend most of that time talking."

"About men?"

"And other things."

"So what did they say about me?"

Slow heat rose from the center of her chest. "You're too conceited by half. If I tell you, you'll be downright unbearable."

His gorgeous face darkened in a scowl. "You think I'm conceited?"

She couldn't help but laugh. "Yes," she said, "actually I do." Although at least he had just cause, which was more than she could say about some of the men she'd known.

"So what did they say?" he persisted.

Something sharp nipped its way down her spine. Jealousy? Impossible. "Pretty much what you'd expect," she said, striving to sound more casual than she felt. "Great face. Great abs. Lousy marriage material."

"Can't argue that."

"No," she said evenly, "you can't."

"I never left anyone standing at the altar."

She looked at him. "I never said you did."

"I wanted you to know."

"I don't know why."

I do, he thought. And that was the hell of it.

Friday

JENNA WOKE UP with a start. Her head rested against Chase's broad chest, and his arm was draped securely across her shoulders as he held her close. She couldn't have been more surprised if she'd awakened in a shark tank wearing a bait necklace.

"Chase." She tapped him on the shoulder. "Wake up, Chase."

He mumbled something then pulled her closer. It felt too good to be safe. She placed a hand against his chest and sat up straight.

"Chase, it's morning. We fell asleep in the car."

He awakened slowly, fighting reality every step of the way. "Nothing's changed, has it?"

She shook her head. "I don't think so."

But she knew better than that. Everything had.

Her heart was expanding inside her chest like a late-blooming flower, petal by petal, opening wide for the sun.

But he's not the right man, Jenna. He'll leave the way the rest of them did.

Still, he touched her in a way no other man ever had, called to a part of her she'd shared with no one.

She was a survivor. She knew how to pick herself up, dust herself off and get on with life. Despite everything—the loss of her parents, the foster homes, the men who said goodbye—there was a core of optimism deep inside her soul that ran deep, and it was that core of optimism that had kept her going when loneliness threatened to pull her under.

You know about loneliness, don't you, Chase? She resisted the urge to brush a lock of hair from his forehead. *We're more alike than either one of us would care to admit.*

Which was another reason why this whole thing had to end before someone got hurt.

There wasn't time to drive home and change before her nine o'clock appointment with the friendly neighborhood banker who owned seventy-five percent of Fantasy Weddings. Jenna and Chase stopped first at a convenience store where she bought a toothbrush and toothpaste then headed for McDonald's to grab breakfast and avail herself of the ladies' room.

As it was she made it to the bank with only a minute to spare.

THE BANKER'S beady little eyes lit up when Jenna glided into the room. Chase found his hands curling into fists at his sides.

"Always a pleasure, Jenna," said the banker.

She shook his hand and took the seat he held out for her. "Your call surprised me," she said. "Is there a problem with the loan?"

"Nothing major." The damn snake couldn't take his eyes off Jenna's legs. "We need Mavis's signature on a few more papers, just to tie up a few loose ends."

"So why didn't he call Mavis?" Chase muttered. "What the hell's he doing bothering you?"

Jenna, who had been wondering the same thing, maintained her composure. "Were you unable to reach Mavis?"

The banker's eyes twinkled. "You know me, Jenna. Can't resist the chance to chat with a pretty woman." He paused a moment, waiting for her reaction. She refused to give him the satisfaction. "I thought you might drop these papers off at her place. She can get a notary to witness her signature."

She wanted to take those papers and stuff them up his nose. Instead she reached for a piece of paper and a pen, then wrote out Mavis's address and pushed it toward the banker. "I'm afraid I won't be seeing Mavis for a while, but you might try FedEx."

Head high, she walked out the door.

"TALK ABOUT a bad attitude," Chase said as she drove from the bank to Fantasy Weddings. "The guy's a patronizing jerk."

"He's a banker," she said. "It comes with the territory."

"Is that the kind of crap women have to put up with?"

"Yeah," she said dryly, "and sometimes it's even unpleasant."

"It gets worse than that?"

"Where have you been the last twenty years, Chase, under a rock? What do you think the fighting has been about?"

How could he tell her that none of it had seemed real or important to him until he saw her square her shoulders and face down a man who wasn't fit to shine her shoes?

She angled the VW into a parking space a few minutes before eleven.

"I'm falling behind in everything," she said over her shoulder as she ran for the door. "Why don't you go wander around the Liberace Museum or something?"

"I thought we'd save that for the honeymoon."

She sighed. "The last time I spent this much time with another human being I was *in utero.*"

He followed her down the hallway to her office.

It was easier to shake a cocklebur from a knit dress than it was to shake Chase Quinn from her side.

Once settled down, she thumbed through the mail piled high in the in basket.

He threw himself into the leather chair by the window and tapped his foot.

"You're not going to sit there all day, are you?" she asked, looking at him over the electric bill.

"Jenna?" Liz appeared in the doorway. "Who are you talking to?"

Jenna managed a smile. "The electric company," she said, studiously ignoring Chase. "Maybe we should've considered solar energy."

Liz stepped inside. "That bad?" She returned Jenna's smile, but it was easy to see the concern behind it.

"That bad," said Jenna.

Liz's smile faded. "Are you okay? I called you last night to ask you how you liked lunch with Donald."

"Yeah," said Chase. "Tell her about lunch with Donald."

She ignored his comment. Practice apparently did make perfect. "Sorry I missed your call, Liz, but I turned off the phone so I could get some sleep."

"Isn't Donald delightful?"

"That isn't quite the word I'd use."

Liz stepped into the room and stood near the leather sofa where Chase was reclining. "You didn't like Donald?" She made it sound like Jenna had declared her hatred of Mom and apple pie.

"I think it was mutual."

"That's not possible." Liz leaned against the arm of the couch. Her behind wasn't six inches away from Chase's propped-up feet. "Donald likes *everyone.*"

"Everyone but me," Jenna said, staring at a disaster in the making. "He split before lunch."

Liz shifted position. So did Chase. Feet and derriere were closer than ever. "A business emergency?"

"He's an accountant, Liz, not a brain surgeon," Jenna reminded her. "If you must know, your poster boy for sensitive men left me standing by the shark tank and ran for his life.''

Liz stared at her in shock. "Not Donald!"

"*Yes*, Donald. I had to buy my own lunch."

And that's when it happened. Liz sank down onto the sofa and let out a scream.

"Watch where you're sitting, lady!" Chase pulled his feet out from under her, and Liz tumbled forward. Jenna reached her just in time.

"You like this sofa?" Liz asked, glaring at the offending piece of furniture.

"I used to," Jenna said, helping her to her feet.

"It's like sitting on a bed of rocks."

"I'm going to get rid of it," Jenna said. "You'll help me pick out a new one."

Liz aimed another nasty look at the sofa. Chase glared back at her, rubbing his right ankle. Jenna wished the floor would open up and devour sofa, receptionist and invisible groom.

"I'm worried about you, Jen."

"Because I have bad taste in furniture?"

Liz waved her hand in the air. "I'm not talking about the furniture. It's something—" She frowned. "Isn't that the same thing you wore yesterday?"

"So it is," she said lightly. "Guess I could use a vacation."

"How about a honeymoon?" Chase offered from across the room.

"Why don't you mind your own business?" she snapped before she had a chance to think.

"Oh, Jenna!" Liz ran from the room in tears.

"See what you did?" Jenna turned on Chase. "You made me hurt Liz's feelings again."

"Want me to go apologize to her?"

She shot him a look that would have hobbled a lesser man. "I want you to stay out of my business."

"Marriage," he said, settling back on the sofa. "Is it great or what?"

It took an hour for Jenna to make amends to Liz, clear up a bookkeeping error with Grace, then eyeball a potential defect in Elvis and Marilyn Monroe. Chase was practicing card tricks in a corner of her office.

"Has anyone heard from Rosalia?" she asked Liz.

Liz shook her head. "I called the apartment three times but got the machine."

"We could use her today," Jenna said. "She's the best at detail work."

"What about her mom's place?" Liz asked. "I didn't try there."

"Of course," said Jenna. "I'll call her." The only way Rosalia was going to break away from Gil permanently was if she established a solid financial footing for herself, and Jenna was determined to do anything she could to make that possible.

Rosalia answered the phone on the second ring.

"We need you, Rosie. We're swamped with work."

"I can't talk, Jenna."

"Rosalia? I can barely hear you."

Silence.

"We have a problem with the plasticine on two of the statues," Jenna went on. "If you could come in today, I'd pay you double time."

Another silence, then, "This is Gil's day off. I have to clean the house."

"But you're at your mom's."

"I know."

"He's standing next to you, isn't he?"

"Yes."

Jenna heard a muffled sound, followed by a sharp intake of breath. "Rosalia, are you okay?"

"I can't talk now," the girl said then hung up.

"What's wrong?" Chase asked, looking up from some intricate maneuver he was practicing.

She sank into her chair and rested her head in her hands. "Life," she said. "Rosalia is young and beautiful and talented and she's about to waste it all on a man who uses her as his own personal punching bag."

"Stay out of it," Chase said.

"I can't stay out of it."

"She's a grown woman. She can make her own decisions."

"She's barely nineteen. I care what happens to her."

"That guy she's with is dangerous."

"Darn right he is," Jenna said, massaging her temples with her fingertips. "I want to make sure Rosalia gets away from Gil before something really dreadful happens."

"I'm not talking about Rosalia," he said. "I'm talking about you."

"Me?" She looked over at him. "I'm not in any danger."

"You will be if you don't back off."

"Gil doesn't pose any threat to me."

"The hell he doesn't. As long as he thinks you're coming between him and Rosalia, you're the enemy."

She tried to ignore the feeling of unease that settled over her like a cold, wet fog. "That's my business, Chase, not yours."

"I saw the way he pushed you in the studio the other day."

She pushed back from the desk and rose to her feet. "You saw *what?*" She remembered her last encounter with Gil quite clearly, and he'd never laid a hand on her.

He swung his legs to the floor and met her eyes. "I saw him grab you."

"But that's not possible. That was last week. You weren't around last week."

"I was here," he said. "You just couldn't see me."

Her heart double-thumped inside her chest. "You mean you were *watching* me?"

"In the studio most of the time. You spent a lot of time working on my...assets."

She gripped the edge of the desk for support. "That was almost two weeks ago." Three times she'd slept in the studio. Good grief, had he seen her naked?

"Took you long enough to realize I was here. I think it was the champagne that finally did it."

"You had no business spying on me."

"I wasn't spying on you."

"You were watching me without my knowledge."

"I was trying to get your attention. It's not my fault you couldn't see me."

"You told me marriage would break the curse." She waved her hands in the air, feeling the last of her control slipping away. "You lied."

"Hey, if it makes you feel any better, I'm having as lousy a time as you are."

"Well, that makes me feel just great. If this is what marriage is all about, I'm glad my other fiancés jilted me."

"I've been meaning to ask you about them."

"They're none of your business."

"I'm the one who didn't run away. That makes them my business."

"Doesn't the word 'jilted' tell you something?"

"Yeah," he said, "but it doesn't explain why you're not brokenhearted."

"Maybe I am brokenhearted," she said, wondering how it was a stranger could see so clearly into her soul.

"You're not," he said, rising to his feet and striding toward her. "You didn't love any of them, did you?"

"What if I didn't?" She lifted her chin with unconscious defiance. "Friendship is every bit as important in a marriage. Maybe even more so."

"And that's why they jilted you."

She felt the sharp sting of tears but willed them away. "I'm not going to have this conversation."

"Why?" he asked, gripping her by the forearms. "Because nobody's ever had the guts to spell it out for you before?"

She tried to pull away but he held her fast. "You wouldn't understand friendship between a man and a woman."

"Friendship didn't get you to the altar, did it?"

"You bastard!"

"You're right," he said. "I *am* a bastard. I'm everything you don't want or need in a husband, but I'll tell you one thing, Jenna—I wouldn't have left you for another woman."

It happened so quickly she didn't have time to react. The pull between them was so violent, so intense, that instinct overruled logic before logic even had a chance. She plunged her hands into his thick, silky hair, tracing the contours of his proud skull with her fingertips. She knew everything there was to know about him, every muscle, every plane, but not even her imagination had prepared her for the warm flesh of a living, breathing man.

His mouth found the hollow of her throat and he touched his tongue to the pulse beating there. She felt as if she were about to go up in flames. His hands caressed her waist, the outward flare of her hips, then slid down her thighs, lifting her skirt up inch by inch until his fingers found the bare skin of her legs.

Her bones melted and she leaned into him, as much for support as for the savage wonder of his touch.

"I don't want to be your friend," she murmured against his hard mouth.

"Good." The sound was almost a growl.

She ripped open his shirt with eager hands. The buttons scattered across the floor. She wanted him naked. She wanted to run her tongue along every swollen, powerful inch of his body, that magnificent body she'd created with her own hands. Her own heart.

And he had ideas of his own. Wondrous ideas. Ideas that made her hot and wet against his hand as he cupped her through the delicate silk of her panties. She imagined his mouth against her and a moan tore from her throat.

"Jenna!" Grace's voice rang out from the next office. "Did you say something?"

Reality was a slap in the face.

"N-no, I didn't," she called out in an abnormally husky voice.

"Sorry," Grace trilled. "My mistake."

Chase found her nipple with his thumb. "Close the door."

"I can't do that. She'll be suspicious. They all will."

"I'm not the one they'll see if they find us."

"This is insane," she whispered. "I don't know what happened to me."

"Yes, you do."

"I'm not usually— I mean, I've never felt . . ." She let her words trail away.

"Three fiancés," he reminded her. "And not one of them—"

She shook her head. "Not one."

"Then you're lucky they took a hike."

Her palms rested against his chest, a barrier between them. "I want something safe, something simple." A man she could count on, not one who courted danger and made his living from illusions.

"I want a home and a family. I want to know where I'll be twenty years from now." *I don't want to be alone.* Dear God, she was so tired of being alone.

"And you don't want this?"

The kiss was shattering in its intensity. A soul-searing reminder of everything that was missing from her life . . . and of all the reasons it had to stay that way.

"No." She broke away from his embrace. "I don't want this." *Liar! You want him more than you've ever wanted anything in your entire life.*

And he knew she was lying. She could see it in his face, the way his eyes lingered on her mouth, as if he sensed rather than heard the words she would never say.

Chapter Ten

By lunchtime, Chase realized there was only one thing left they could do to possibly break the curse that was ruining both of their lives.

"That's crazy!" Jenna said when he told her about his plan.

"It's either that or you get used to having me around twenty-four hours a day, seven days a week, for the rest of your life."

"I'll do it." The expression on her beautiful face spoke volumes. Her eagerness bruised his ego. "I don't like it, but I'll do it."

They couldn't continue the way they were. The tension between them was sharp as the blade of a knife, and he knew it was only a matter of time before it drew first blood. He wanted her, and he'd come close to taking her right there in her office. The only thing that had stopped him was the look of vulnerability in her eyes, a sadness that struck a chord in him he'd forgotten ever existed.

JENNA AND CHASE got married for the second time that day at three o'clock in the main chapel. The Ten Pins, a world champion coed bowling team from Flagstaff, Arizona, had decided to celebrate their latest victory by renewing their respective wedding vows.

"We'll stand in the back," Jenna said, "and repeat the vows with them."

"What about the paperwork?"

"All we have to do is sign an affidavit stating we're already married to each other."

"Are we married to each other?"

"Thanks to Mavis we are." *Married,* she thought with amazement. *I'm a married woman.*

"Maybe this time we'll manage to break the curse."

"From your mouth to God's ear."

He waggled his eyebrows at her in a comic leer. "A temporary marriage might have a few enjoyable perks."

She ignored him but knew that the high color in her cheeks was answer enough. Not even she could deny the fiercely volatile chemistry between the two of them. It was everything she'd known it would be. She'd been right to avoid him when they both worked at the Paradise Hotel.

There was nothing safe or secure about Chase Quinn. You couldn't count on him to be there when the going got tough or you got old or life sent heartache your way. Men like Chase took pleasure where they found it then went on their way.

She understood that. She accepted that. She'd avoided him like the plague.

Who would have imagined that fate, in its dubious wisdom, would one day bring them together as husband and wife?

Even the second time around she couldn't quite believe it was happening.

"I'll oversee this one," she said to Liz, pretending all was business as usual.

"You did the last one," Liz protested. "Let me take it."

"The buck stops here," she said lightly. "Forty happy couples sound like a job for the boss."

"She gets more suspicious every time you open your mouth," Chase said as he walked with her down the hall. "She thinks you're acting weird."

"I am acting weird," Jenna whispered. "She still thinks I'm mad at her."

"She'll get over it."

"I hope so."

"Jenna." Grace popped out of the ladies' room. "Who are you talking to?"

"Myself." It wasn't true but it was the only answer anyone could possibly believe.

"Oh." Grace's eyes widened. "Okay."

"Way to go," Chase said, chuckling. "Not much she can say to that."

Jenna ignored him. She could feel Grace's eyeballs burning a hole in her back as she strode toward the chapel. She had the distinct feeling that if one more person caught her talking to herself, she'd be bundled off to a rubber room.

The justice of the peace was settling his glasses on the bridge of his nose when Jenna and Chase stepped into the chapel. The forty happy couples, all clad in bright yellow bowling shirts, beamed at him expectantly.

To her horror, Jenna's eyes welled with tears as she took her place at the back of the room.

"You're crying," Chase observed. "You didn't cry at our last wedding."

"Look at them," she whispered. "They're so happy."

The justice of the peace cleared his throat. "As I was saying," he intoned with a quelling look aimed at Jenna, "the bonds of matrimony are..."

She sniffled loudly and wiped her eyes with the back of her hand.

Chase grabbed a tissue from the dispenser to the right of the door.

"Here." He extended the tissue toward Jenna.

"Renewing vows made in the sweetness of youth— Good God in heaven! Am I seeing things?"

Forty pairs of eyes turned toward Jenna. The tissue! It must look like it was floating through space. She reached for it and quickly dabbed at her eyes. "I must remember to turn down the air conditioner," she said. "There's quite a draft in here."

The ceremony resumed.

"Do that again," she whispered to Chase, "and I'll shoot you."

"Hell of a way to talk on your wedding day."

"If there is just cause that these men and these women shall not be joined together again in matrimony—"

She looked at her hands. She'd never been one for fancy jewelry, but suddenly she imagined a plain gold band, could feel the weight of it on her finger, the rightness of it.

Chase reached for her left hand and held it between his own.

Don't do this, she thought. *Don't try to make this ceremony something it isn't.*

But she didn't break the connection.

"Repeat after me..."

A huge lump of emotion lodged in Jenna's throat, and try as she might she couldn't make it go away.

"I, Jenna, take you, Chase—"

Don't cry, he thought. *This wasn't supposed to make you cry.* This ceremony was a means to an end, nothing more.

"I, Chase, take you, Jenna—"

A ring, he thought. A marriage wasn't complete without a ring. Maybe that's where they'd gone wrong. He looked at the silver band on his right hand. He'd bought that ring with the first money he made with his magic. It was his talisman, his good luck piece. He tugged it off his finger.

"No!" Jenna pulled away. "You can't."

"Quiet." His voice was gruff as he slipped the heavy silver band onto the middle finger of her left hand.

"By the power vested in me by the good state of Nevada, I now pronounce you all once again men and wives." The justice of the peace removed his glasses and offered one and all a wide, myopic smile. "Gentlemen, you may kiss your brides!"

The chapel exploded with laughter and delighted cheers. Forty husbands gathered forty wives into their arms and planted exuberant kisses on their familiar lips.

Chase bent to kiss his own bride.

"Stop!" Jenna hissed. "He's watching."

"Let him," said Chase as he found her mouth with his.

It wasn't much as kisses went, a fleeting second of contact that was over before it started. Yet it mattered in a way the more heated, passionate kisses of the night before hadn't.

"Jenna." His voice caressed her.

Her mouth curved in a smile. "Chase."

She felt a flutter of something new and wonderful inside her chest, but it flew away before she could capture it.

"This is it," Chase said as the justice of the peace made his way toward them. "The moment of truth."

"Wonderful job," Jenna said, smiling as she shook the man's hand. "I have the paperwork in my office for you to sign."

The man nodded, his expression never wavering. "You are a most peculiar woman, Ms. Grey. A most peculiar woman. For a moment I thought you were kissing someone, but it's plain to see there's no one here."

"What an odd notion!" She chuckled as if she hadn't a care in the world. "I think we've all been bitten by the wedding bug."

"Damn." Chase waved a hand in front of the man's pointed nose. "He can't see me."

She looked at Chase, then at the justice of the peace. No doubt about it. The older man had no idea Chase stood next to him. Elation and disappointment battled for dominance, and elation won, hands down.

That fact scared her more than the IRS, Armageddon and cellulite combined. There was nothing between them, certainly nothing that mattered.

But there was something exciting about it all, something thrilling and dangerous and so *right* that she had to turn away so her husband wouldn't see her smile.

HE WAS THINKING about her smile when it happened. One second he was contemplating the way the left side of her mouth was punctuated with a dimple, and the next second he was propelled backward into an abyss where there was no light, no sound, nothing but the knowledge that he'd never see her again.

This wasn't like the times when he'd fade out in front of her but was there in all the other ways that mattered. He sensed the pull of darkness, knew that if he gave in for even a moment, everything he was, everything he ever could be, would be gone forever.

And then, in the blink of an eye, he was standing next to her again while the minister droned on about what a peculiar woman Jenna was.

A warning, he thought, as he followed her to her office. A reminder that time was running out, and so far there was nothing he could do to stop it.

As a courtesy for both employees and patrons, Fantasy Weddings maintained a small hotel-style buffet. Jenna waited for a break then grabbed two large dinner plates. Shrimp salad, barbecued chicken, pepper steak with onions, a pair of pasta dishes. She was reaching for the Italian bread when she sensed someone watching her.

Unfortunately it wasn't Chase.

"Jenna?" Liz's brows were knotted over the bridge of her nose. "What on earth—"

Jenna glanced at the mountains of food on her plates, then at her friend. "What can I say? Buffets are my downfall."

"You're not going to eat all of that, are you?"

"I was going to give it my best shot."

Poor Liz. Jenna could only hope her own emotions weren't as visible on her face.

"Do you eat like this very often?" Liz asked.

"I, um, I..."

Liz placed a comforting hand on Jenna's forearm. "I used to binge, too, Jenna, but Weight Minders taught me how to make better choices." She took the plates from Jenna and placed them on the sideboard. "Let me show you a better way..."

"This stinks," Chase said, pushing an alfalfa sprout salad around on his paper plate. "I know goats who wouldn't eat this swill."

It was impossible to vent your anger on an organic cucumber slice. Jenna took a stab at the innocent vegetable and popped it into her mouth, but her action lacked the dramatic impact she was seeking. It was times like this that made her understand why humankind was carnivorous.

"You don't really like this stuff, do you?"

She refused to meet his eyes. "As a matter of fact, I do."

He took a mouthful of alfalfa sprouts. "It's like chewing on sawdust."

Jenna's nerves were at the breaking point. Her emotions shifted like the desert winds, blowing alternately hot and cold, keeping her off guard and vulnerable. One minute she was growing weepy over their second—or was it third?—wedding ceremony, and the next she wanted to hit him over the head with innocent vegetables.

In less than two days her entire life had been turned upside down and she was reasonably sure she was about to lose what was left of her mind.

Liz thought she had a terrible eating disorder and was volunteering to sponsor her at the next Weight Minders meeting. Grace had overheard the conversation and offered the name of her hypnotherapist, a brilliant man who could make you think broccoli was a hot fudge sundae. Before long they'd be padlocking the fridge and monitoring her consumption of diet cola.

And all because of the man sitting before her, grimacing over his alfalfa sprouts.

She groaned and rested her head on the desk. "This has to be the worst two days of my entire life."

"Just what a bridegroom loves to hear."

"I wish you wouldn't say things like that. There's nothing funny about this situation."

"Don't worry," he said. "Less than forty-eight hours and it's all over... one way or another."

She looked at him over the mound of vegetables on her plate. "I'm not sure I believe you."

"You'll find out soon enough."

She rose from her chair, hands braced on the top of her desk. "I can't believe you're going to *die* if our marriage doesn't take."

"Like I told you before, that's what the man said."

"You're scaring me." Unseen voices were right up there with things that went bump in the night.

"Scared the hell out of me the first time."

She thought of the heat between them and wondered how much of it had been Chase's idea and how much had been orchestrated by someone else's hand. "So we're not alone."

His eyes darkened as he looked at her. "We're alone."

"How can you be so sure?"

"I haven't heard the voice since the night you drank too much cheap wine."

"That was champagne," she corrected him, "and it wasn't cheap."

"It might as well have come with a screw top for all you noticed. You were gulping that stuff like soda."

"I can't believe we're even having this conversation."

"I can't believe we're married."

"Me, neither." She held up her left hand with the heavy silver ring on the middle finger. "Except for this, I still don't feel any different."

"Why would you feel different?"

"Because marriage is important—or at least it should be. I always thought everything would change once I said those words."

"Maybe this is all there is," he persisted. He'd seen how little marriage mattered to his mother, and nothing he'd observed in the years since had proven otherwise. "You find somebody, you say the words in front of a preacher, and you go on doing whatever it was you were doing before."

"You saw the couples in the chapel. Saying those words meant something to them." She had spent her life believing in the miracle of two souls finding each other against the odds, then uniting their hearts and minds in marriage. Maybe it would never happen for her, but she had to believe it was possible for someone, somewhere.

His expression was shadowed. "They're bowlers. Hitting a seven-ten split means something to them."

"You know, you're not as tough as you pretend to be."

"I'm tougher."

"I'm not so certain."

"I'm not one of those brokenhearted guys you specialize in. Save the pop psychology for someone who needs it."

She didn't argue the point with him. He *was* as tough as they came, hard-bodied, strong-minded, needing no one and making sure no one needed him.

But, tough as he was, he needed her.

She wished that fact didn't matter quite as much as it did.

JENNA AND CHASE squeezed in a third wedding later that evening. A pair of twin sisters married twin chiropractors in a raucous rock and roll ceremony presided over by a preacher in a spangled Elvis jumpsuit. Jenna and her invisible groom stood in the shadows and repeated their vows and waited once again for something, anything, to happen.

Of course nothing did.

"Look at them," Chase said, gesturing toward the eager brides and grooms. "Don't they know they stand a snowball's chance in hell of making it work?"

Jenna's expression went all soft and dreamy. "They're in love. Love makes it all seem possible."

"I give them a year," he said, trying to ignore the jabs of hope poking him in the chest. "Maybe only six months."

"I think they're going to make it," Jenna said, dabbing at her eyes. "See the way they're looking at each other? That's the real thing."

"It always *looks* like the real thing in the beginning. That's how the trouble starts."

"Love isn't trouble," she protested. "It's what makes life worth living."

"I've done fine without it."

"Right," she said, shaking her head. "Cursed, alone and invisible. You're doing just great."

Elvis snapped shut his prayer book and gyrated for the assembled throng. "Thank you, thank you very much. Now, ya'll can kiss the brides."

Chase and Jenna didn't kiss this time. Truth was, they didn't need to. The memory of their last kiss still danced in the air between them, heightening the absurd situation in which they found themselves.

"We're both cursed," she said as she swept up the rice and discarded the streamers. "This nightmare is never going to end.'' She said the words, but suddenly she wasn't certain she believed them the way she had a few hours ago.

''It'll end,'' he said in an ominous tone of voice. ''Two more days and I'm history.''

''I'm going out to the studio and start repairing Marilyn and Elvis.''

Chase stifled a yawn. ''When are we going home?''

''We?'' She arched a brow. ''We're married, but I didn't think we were planning to live together.''

He shrugged then stifled another yawn. ''Don't you ever get tired?'' As far as he could tell, she'd been awake almost forty-eight hours.

''I'm exhausted,'' she admitted, ''but with Rosalia out, someone has to do the repair work.''

''Let it wait.''

''I can't. The local newspaper's sending a photographer over tomorrow for the Sunday supplement and I want everything to be perfect.''

''Do you have a sofa in the studio?''

She nodded.

''Great,'' he said, heading for the door. ''Let's go.''

''I'm a private person.'' She barred his exit. ''We've been together for almost two days straight. I need some time to myself.''

''You can't always get what you want,'' he said dryly. ''That's why they call it a curse.''

She opened the door and stepped outside. Chase was close behind.

"You're going to be bored," she tossed over her shoulder as they crossed the parking lot. "Repair work is very tedious."

"I won't be bored. I'll be asleep."

He was as good as his word. She'd barely reintroduced herself to Elvis before Chase was catching Zs on the tiny sofa pushed up against the back wall.

"Sleep well," she mumbled. The man was an expert at it, although how he could manage to sleep with his legs hanging over one side and his shaggy head drooping over the other was beyond Jenna. His arms were folded across his chest, and for an instant she felt a bittersweet rush of longing so deep, so profound, that she had to turn away.

Don't even think it. So what if he was her husband. So what if they'd taken their vows three times in less than twenty-four hours. That didn't change the fact that this was a ridiculous situation and the smartest thing she could do was get out while the getting was good.

If only she could figure out how.

Chapter Eleven

Chase woke up to find his wife crouched on the floor with a crowbar wedged between the jamb and the door. From the look of things, she was applying enough force to break into your average bank vault. If the situation had been any less bizarre he might have felt insulted, but all things considered, he supposed he couldn't blame her.

He swung his feet to the floor and stood up. "Need a hand over there?"

She dropped the crowbar with a thud. "You're awake!"

"What did you expect with all that grunting and groaning going on?"

"I wasn't grunting and groaning."

"The hell you weren't. I thought you were doing your aerobics."

She tossed her mane of dark hair off her face then met his eyes. "If you must know, I was trying to escape."

"That's what I thought."

"It's nothing personal," she said, "but I just can't take this anymore. I'd rather be having a root canal. I feel like my whole life is out of control and I hate it!"

Damn it, Chase thought as her chin began to tremble. Didn't it figure she'd go and get weepy on him. He'd never met a woman who knew how to fight fair. Her blue eyes swam with tears, although he noted she managed to blink them back before a single one trailed its way down her cheek. And it was a good thing. Even though he knew all about illusions and how nothing was exactly the way it seemed, there was still something about a woman's tears that had the power to turn his heart into mush.

Something that made him stop thinking and start feeling.

"C'mon," he said gruffly, fighting the urge to gather her to him and hold her close. "It's not so bad."

"It's terrible. It's worse than terrible."

"Easy on the flattery. You don't want to turn my head."

"It's almost midnight and I'm standing here talking to a man no one else on earth can see or hear. I've been up for days on end and I'm ready to fall on my face." He could see that she regretted her momentary loss of control and was reconstructing her defenses as quickly as she could manage. "I don't know how we're going to work all of this out but I have to get some sleep before I go crazy."

He thought of that big wide bed of hers, piled high with comforters and pillows. "Sounds good to me."

"Not in this lifetime."

"You're a suspicious woman, Jenna Grey," he said, shaking his head. "You've got to learn to trust people."

"Right," she said. "When pigs fly."

THE IRONY OF IT was that she couldn't sleep. After the tirade she'd delivered about her exhaustion, sleep continued to elude her.

There she was, barricaded in her bedroom as if Chase were an opposing army ready to strike at a moment's notice, when the truth was, he'd been nothing but kind and considerate and distant.

It was the distance that disturbed her. She had the sense that a barrier had suddenly popped up between them. She couldn't see it or touch it, but it was there and growing larger every minute. Was his time as limited as he'd said it was? She didn't want to believe it but she feared it might be true.

A deep sadness filled her soul. He didn't even look the same, she thought, as she lay in the darkness, staring at the ceiling. In the car on the way home she'd imagined she could see right through him, as if he were nothing but a figment of her imagination and not a living, breathing man at all.

Totally illogical, she knew, but along about the first wedding ceremony she'd stopped looking for logic.

Along about the second wedding ceremony she'd stopped praying for success.

By the third wedding ceremony she'd actually begun to enjoy herself, and that scared her more than anything.

She had no business enjoying herself. This was a no-win situation as it had been from the start. She should be poring through reference books, calling psychics, praying on her hands and knees for a way to break the curse on Quinn. Instead she was lying in bed alone, entertaining fantasies that a sane woman would recognize for what they were—the evidence of incipient madness.

She reached for the phone and punched in Mavis's number.

Mavis was her cheery night-owl self, acting as if a middle-of-the-night phone call was business as usual. "How are the newlyweds?"

Jenna sighed loudly. "Togetherness isn't all it's cracked up to be."

"There's togetherness and then there's *togetherness*." Jenna could imagine the older woman's eyebrows waggling in emphasis. "Marriage without sex is like being the only vegetarian at a butchers' picnic."

"Wonderful analogy, Mavis, but I don't see what it has to do with us. You know this isn't a real marriage."

"Honey, you two have enough electricity to light Caesar's Palace."

"We're not a love match, Mavis. We're not even friends."

Mavis was undaunted. "I always knew you two would find each other. Didn't I tell you that he was the one for you?"

"I wish you wouldn't say things like that! We didn't find each other. He showed up on my doorstep."

"You wanted him and he came to you."

"I didn't want him." She caught herself. "I mean, I *don't* want him." Mavis's silence was telling. "Don't do this to me, Mavis! I didn't ask for him and he certainly didn't choose me. It all just...happened."

"I don't know much, honey, but the one thing I do know is that nothing in this life just happens. It's all part of a great big plan. You and that handsome young man have been handed something real special and now it's up to you to do something with it."

"If it's so special, why do I feel so miserable?"

"That's exactly how you're supposed to feel."

"I didn't feel miserable before he showed up."

"You felt lonely." The older woman's voice softened. "Bet you're not feelin' so lonely now."

Jenna wanted to deny the truth but couldn't. "Who has time to feel lonely?" she countered lightly. "We're stuck together like two pieces of Velcro."

"It's what we all pray for, honey. Nobody wants to be alone. That ain't the way we're meant to go through life. Want me to tell you all about why I've married so many men?"

"I'd rather you tell me how I can break the curse, get an annulment and get on with my life."

"Honey, if I could do that I'd be givin' Ann Landers a run for her money."

"What am I going to do, Mavis? I want my life back the way it was."

"Maybe you should stop fightin' so hard and take another look at what you've got right under your nose. Happiness don't come around too many times in life, honey. Ask the old ones...we know."

"The whole world's gone crazy," Jenna said as she placed the receiver on its cradle. Invisible men, multiple weddings, Mavis's certainty that Jenna and Chase were a match made in curse-meister heaven. If there was one thread of sanity in the crazy quilt her life had become, she couldn't find it.

She lay back in bed and closed her eyes. Her bedroom door was locked from the inside, and unless the man could walk through walls she was perfectly safe. Perfectly alone.

Or was she? For all she knew he could be standing right there by the head of her bed, watching her with those deep gold eyes of his. Eyes that saw everything and revealed nothing at all.

What was that Mavis had said about happiness, that it didn't come around too many times in life? The words had struck an unexpected chord in Jenna. She'd been waiting twenty-six years to be happy... could this be her one and only chance?

Chase was a stranger... and her husband. They'd married each other three times, yet she knew more about her cleaning lady than she did about the man who'd given her the silver ring she wore on her left hand.

This wasn't the way it was supposed to be. Not even Mavis could say that. None of Jenna's daydreams about her wedding night had included sleeping alone, being alone.

Maybe this was the only wedding night she would ever have and the man sleeping on her sofa was the only husband she'd ever know. Ten or twenty years from now she might look back on this night and wonder how it was she'd decided that sleeping alone behind a locked door was the better part of valor.

Right now it only seemed a pathetic waste of time.

She moved through the hallway as if in a dream. She heard the gentle tick of the mantel clock in the living room as she approached. She didn't know what she was going to say to him or what she was going to do. All she knew was that she was so tired of being alone, so tired of waiting for the rest of her life to begin that the longing inside her heart was a physical ache.

CHASE STOOD at the window and looked out at the quiet street. Moonlight bounced off the hoods of Chevys and Hyundais and dirt bikes abandoned for the night. If someone had asked him a few years ago where he thought he'd be tonight, he might have said Paris or Rome or even the stage of the Paradise Hotel, but he never would have said 524 Sagebrush Lane.

But there he was, a married man with nothing to show for his change of status except for a signed marriage certificate and a sense of disappointment that shook him right down to his shoes.

"So what are you disappointed about?" he said to the empty room. To be disappointed you had to have expectations, and from the moment he found himself trapped in the old Tucker Mine, his expectations had been limited to reclaiming what was left of his life.

But not any longer. He damned the forces that had brought him to this place and time. He knew the kind of woman Jenna was. She wanted things he didn't even think about, home and family and love. Prickly, beautiful Jenna with the razor-sharp wit and the show girl's body and the generous heart that should never have been broken. At least that was one thing he wouldn't do. She'd never let him close enough, and maybe that was the best thing for both of them.

"Chase."

Her voice was soft as his dreams, the same dreams he'd been avoiding from the first moment he saw her face. He turned slowly, delaying the moment of inevitability. And it was inevitable, as inevitable as his next breath, as inevitable as the fact that he wanted her in a way other men wanted freedom and power.

She wore a cotton nightgown that brushed her ankles. Her hair was pulled back from her face and tied with a piece of sapphire blue ribbon. She looked younger without makeup, more vulnerable, yet the sheer force of her beauty still affected him like a blow.

"You should be asleep."

"I tried." She shrugged her shoulders. "Couldn't do it."

"Warm milk," he said, trying to look away but failing.

A smile played at her lips. "Is that what your mother told you?"

"My mother never told me anything."

She moved closer. He wondered if she knew the effect her nearness was having on him. "She must have told you something. Mothers are filled with great advice."

"My mother left when I was five."

"Left?" She placed a hand on his shoulder. "Do you mean she died?"

"I mean she left." The pain was closer to the surface than he would have imagined. "Packed up one day, patted me on the head and took off."

Her eyes glistened in the darkened room. "I'm sorry. That must have been very hard."

He started to deny it the way he'd denied everything his whole damn life, but the lie died in his throat before he could give it voice. "Yeah," he said. "It was hard."

"I know," she whispered.

"You can't know. You're one of the lucky ones." He needed to believe sorrow had never touched her soul.

"Lucky?" Her soft laugh broke his heart. "My parents died when I was thirteen."

"You had other family."

She shook her head. "No one."

"Thirteen." He saw her young and lovely and alone in a world that made it its business to destroy innocence.

"Foster homes," she said, seeing the question in his eyes. "More foster homes than I can count."

"Did your parents love you?" Only someone who'd known the flip side of the fairy tale could ask that question.

"Yes," she whispered. "That only made it harder."

"At least you had that. My mother turned her back on me. My father never forgave her."

"Still you had a father. I would have sold my soul to have just one parent."

"So would I."

"But you said—"

"I've been invisible to my old man for a hell of a long time."

Jenna felt his pain the way she felt her own. Years and years of it, digging down into the center of her soul until there wasn't room for anything else. Ancient instincts were at work, the dark call of sexuality, the healing power of something she didn't dare put a name to but understood in the deepest part of her soul. This was the man she'd waited her entire life to find and she opened her arms to him at the same time she opened her heart.

CHASE WASN'T A MAN given to larger than life gestures unless those gestures were on stage before thousands of adoring fans. He'd been told he had no romance in his soul, that the only real magic he'd ever performed was making people believe he had a heart.

He'd never argued that fact. He knew he wasn't like other men, that deep emotion and strong attachments were not in the cards for him no matter how carefully he stacked the deck.

But at that moment he knew different. A heart was the only logical explanation for the deep ache he felt in the center of his chest as he looked into her eyes.

"You deserve better than this," he said, resisting the urge to pull her into his arms and find release in her softness.

"Let me be the judge of that."

He didn't know what he was waiting for. He didn't know if he was doing the right thing, the wrong thing, or nothing at all. All he knew was that a better man would let her go.

"Nothing lasts," he said, his lips pressed to the hollow of her throat. "Not even this."

Her eyes closed as a wave of warmth washed over her. "I'll take my chances." She'd waited forever for this moment, wondered if she would recognize it when it finally came, needing it more than she needed water or oxygen or food.

He swept her off her feet and she looped her arms about his neck as he carried her through the darkened house toward her bedroom. She buried her face against the side of his neck and breathed deeply of the scent of wood smoke and spice. For the rest of her life she would never be able to smell that intoxicating blend of aromas and not think of this man, this moment. *What if that's all you have of him, Jenna?*

"This is enough," she whispered. It was even more than she'd dreamed.

The faint whisper of her perfume scented the air as he crossed the threshold into her bedroom. A small night-light flickered from the far side of the room, illuminating the gentle shapes of chaise longue and dressing table and bed. The covers were rumpled, as if she'd tossed and turned. The pillows were bunched up against the headboard. He noted the tumble of sheets and comforter, of lace and linen, as he lowered her to the mattress.

Her hair fanned out around her glorious face as she looked up at him with eyes wide with desire. For him. It was enough to make him believe in magic.

And magic was everywhere in that small room that night. Magic was in the way her heart seemed to stop beating as he stripped off his shirt. Magic was in the way he looked at her as he eased her nightgown over her shoulders. Magic was in the thrill of skin against skin, of expectations met, of dreams about to come true.

They lay together on the bed and the world faded away. She knew his body as intimately as she knew her own, and yet all those weeks of working on his statue, of creating the framework of bone, caressing the swell of muscles—none of it had prepared her for the sheer eroticism of movement. Of heat.

She cried out when he cupped her breast with his beautiful, magical hand, and when he brought his mouth to her nipple and suckled, she felt as if she were spinning out to the edge of the universe.

He could hear her heart pounding in the quiet room, could feel the tension in her muscles as he inched his way down her glorious body, over her rib cage, across her belly. He buried his face in the triangle of soft curls and blew softly against her skin. She shuddered in response, her back arching off the bed. He clasped her hips with his hands, and drew his mouth lower still, until he found the swollen lips, the wetness, the sweetness he'd been searching all his life to find.

She bucked wildly against him yet held him fast with her strong thighs. The combination came close to pushing him over the edge, and he had to call on every delaying measure he'd ever heard about to keep from denying them both the ultimate fulfillment.

But he wanted her to take her first pleasure now. He wanted to savor her climax, to know that he was the one—his hands, his mouth—that had given her the transcendent joy she was reaching for.

She heard the cry as if from a great distance, a high, piercing cry that rang out toward the stars, and it took her a moment to realize the cry was her own. She had traveled so far and been gone so long...

He caressed his way back up her body, turning every place he touched into someplace sacred.

She moved restlessly beneath him, shocked by the need gathering again deep inside her body, that ancient need to welcome a man in the most intimate embrace.

His erection burned against her thigh. He took her hand in his, kissed her palm with tenderness that brought sudden tears to her eyes, then placed her hand against his body. Instinctively her fingers curled around him. So powerful, she thought in wonder, yet so amazingly soft. What other miracles had she yet to discover?

The innocence of her touch should have told him, but the fire burning inside his head incinerated everything but the primal urge to bury himself in her softness. He tried to rein in the violence of his need, to tame his hunger, but it was a difficult battle. She was everything he'd ever wanted, all that he had been searching for, the miracle without a name that had existed just beyond reach the whole of his life, and in seconds she would be his.

He moved between her thighs, powerfully aroused by the sight of her naked beneath him, the smell of her skin, the sounds she was making in the back of her throat. He cupped her with his palm, groaning at the fierce wet heat, waiting to ease his way into her body.

"Now." His voice was rough with need.

She pushed against his hand. "Yes . . . oh, God, yes . . ."

He parted her with his hand and slowly began to enter her. When she cried out it took him a second to realize why.

"Don't stop," she said. Her eyes were wide with both desire and fear. "I don't want you to stop."

It wouldn't have mattered if he hadn't been the first, but the fact that he was affected him more deeply than he could have ever known. He wanted her to know how good it could be when it was right. He wanted her to feel what he was feeling at that moment, as if he could touch the sky.

Jenna tensed as he pressed against her body. She knew there would be pain; she assumed there would be pleasure. She never expected there would be such deep, soul-shattering joy. Such a simple act, the union of a man and a woman. Why hadn't anyone ever told her that it was so much more than that?

She welcomed him into her body but she was also taking him inside her soul.

Chase had spent most of his life viewing women as alien creatures from another planet. He'd wooed and bedded them, he'd enjoyed them, but he'd never claimed to understand them. Not until Jenna.

Joined together in the act of love, he had the feeling that he had finally found the other half of his heart. Tangled up with the heat and the passion was the deep certainty that whatever else happened in the next twenty-four hours, he had known a night of joy so deep and powerful that it couldn't be expressed in words. Words were one-dimensional, cold and brittle objects that could never capture her warmth or the wonder she made him feel.

And so he made love to her a second time, with some of the fire banked, some of the urgency tempered, and tried to show her with his mortal body all that was in his heart.

Jenna sensed the difference immediately. The fierce thrill of discovery still heated her blood, but there was something else added, something so strong, so powerful, that it transcended physical pleasure. The way he caressed her was almost sacramental; the way she responded, spiritual. It was as if they had somehow managed to strip away the skin and expose their vulnerable beating hearts.

"Now I feel married," she whispered as the storm receded and they again lay quietly on the shore.

He held her close, smoothing her hair from her forehead, memorizing the sweet curve and angles of her face. Unless they stumbled onto another miracle, in less than twenty-four hours he would be gone.

It was happening. He could feel it in the air around him, in the whisper of destiny sounding inside his head. Time was running out and apparently there was nothing he could do to stop it. Twice in the last few hours he'd seemed to slip from his body, falling backward into that cold blackness that he remembered too well.

Both times he'd been able to battle away from the edge, pull himself out of the abyss at the last moment, drawn to the light by the way she made him feel.

She made him happy.

And at the stroke of midnight even that would be gone.

"I DON'T HAVE TO WORK," Jenna said as dawn swept across the desert. "We can stay in bed all day."

Both felt the bittersweet tug of reality but neither chose to acknowledge it. It was enough that they were together, that they had this moment in time.

He glanced at the clock on the nightstand. "I'll make you breakfast in bed. How does that sound?"

"That sounds wonderful," she said, curling up against his warm body. "Provided you share it with me."

He pulled her closer and kissed her thoroughly. "Try and stop me."

He swung his legs from the bed and stood up.

"Don't," she said as he reached for his jeans.

He met her eyes and grinned. "I thought you had a problem with naked breakfasts."

"I was young," she said, grinning back. "I didn't know any better."

He pulled his jeans on anyway. "You were right about frying bacon," he said, zipping the fly. "Too dangerous." He leaned over and kissed her forehead. "Sleep, Jenna. I'll wake you when breakfast's ready."

He'd made a thousand breakfasts in his life, but he'd never made breakfast for a woman before that morning. The morning after had never held any appeal for him. He was never cruel about it, but once it was over, it was over. Making love was one thing. Making small talk over coffee and toast was something else. Something he had no desire to do.

Until Jenna.

Sex was only a small part of what they'd shared. The thought should have scared the hell out of him but it didn't.

He strode into the kitchen and headed straight for the refrigerator. He was beginning to sound like a romantic cliché straight out of some sappy women's magazine. Next thing you know he'd be tucking love notes under her pillow and sipping champagne from her Reeboks. He grabbed the handle and swung open the door to the refrigerator, only to find himself yanked off his feet, turned end over end, then hurtled backward through what seemed like a narrow tunnel of blackness that was colder than the thought of life without Jenna Grey.

"It's not over yet," he roared when he realized he was back in the old Tucker Mine where it had all begun. "I still have more time."

This is beyond my control, Quinn. It has always been beyond my control.

"I'm not going to stay here. I have to go back."

You are so close to understanding what lies at the heart of life. Do not make the same mistake all over again.

"Damn it! She thinks I'm making breakfast. You can't do this to her—"

One moment he was in the mine. The next moment he was in Jenna's kitchen, reaching for the eggs in the refrigerator. He'd won the battle, but he was afraid he was about to lose the war.

THE BED SMELLED of him... of them. Spice. Shalimar. Sexuality. All the nights she'd spent alone, dreaming of this moment, this man, vanished as if they'd never happened, and a sense of peace and contentment filled her soul.

They would find a way to make this work. She refused to believe something as ridiculous as a curse could tear them apart. Taking their vows hadn't been enough to break the curse, but maybe a *real* marriage, and all that implied, would do the trick.

And she did feel married now. Unexpectedly, inexplicably married. Did he feel that way, too? She knew marriage wasn't part of his life's game plan, but there was no denying that what had happened between them was the stuff of dreams.

Even the mysterious forces that governed things like curses should be able to see that.

Suddenly she couldn't bear being apart from him for another second. Who could say how much—or how little—time they had left together? She leapt from the bed, grabbed her robe from the back of the chaise longue.

"I should smell bacon frying," she called out as she hurried into the kitchen. "Let's rattle those pots and—"

She stopped abruptly. The front burner was on full blast, shooting blue flames into the air. The frying pan was on the floor. An unopened package of bacon rested on the countertop.

"Chase?" She moved to the center of the room. "Are you playing a trick on me?"

She heard a noise and spun around, expecting to see him standing by the entrance with his Kodachrome smile aimed right at her. There was nobody there.

The curse. Maybe—

"No!" The word exploded into the quiet kitchen. Not yet. It was too soon. She wasn't ready to lose him. Not now. Not ever.

"So what's the problem?"

She jumped at the familiar voice behind her left shoulder, near the refrigerator. "Good grief!" She placed a hand over her thudding heart. "Where on earth were you?" He didn't look quite right, but then she wasn't herself at that moment either.

"Burned my hand on the stove," he said in an easy tone. "Went to run cold water on it."

"We have cold water in here, too," she said, moving toward him. "Let me see."

He sidestepped her. "Nothing much to see. The water did the trick." He placed his hands on her shoulders and aimed her toward the hallway. "Back to bed, Jenna. I do my best work without an audience."

She raised up on tiptoe and kissed him full on the mouth. "Oh, no, you don't."

She went back to bed, certain that all was right with the world.

He watched her go, knowing the end was near.

Chapter Twelve

They made love. They ate breakfast. They made love again.

Then, as the sun rose high in the sky, they pulled the drapes tightly closed and lay wrapped in each other's arms. It was life at its most perfect . . . and most temporary.

Chase tried to talk to her about what might be ahead, but Jenna refused to listen.

"Something's wrong," he said, holding her hands between his. "The signs are everywhere."

"Don't be silly," she said with a forced laugh. "You're just tired."

"The curse is unbroken, Jenna. We haven't been able to find a way to turn back the clock. Maybe we never will."

"I don't want to hear this."

"I was pulled back to—"

"Don't say it! I refuse to let you say it."

"Not saying it doesn't mean—"

"Wait and see," she told him fiercely. "I know everything will work out."

They slept through the afternoon and might have slept even later if the telephone hadn't blared.

Jenna pulled the pillow over her ears. "The phone's on your side," she said to Chase. "You answer it."

No response.

"You're impossible," she mumbled. "I'll have to remember to keep the machine on in the future."

Future, she thought, smiling as she reached over his head for the phone. What a wonderful, wonderful word.

She grabbed it on the fifth ring, noticing as she did that his side of the bed was empty. A prickle of apprehension crept in behind her euphoria.

Her hello went unanswered.

"This is getting old, whoever you are. If this is an obscene phone call, you're not getting your message across."

"Jenna."

She cupped her hand around her other ear and strained to listen. "Rosalia?"

"I need your . . . help."

Her delight was tempered by concern. "Anything, Rosie. Just tell me what you need and it's yours."

"He hurt me, Jenna." Her voice was a whisper. "I'm . . . hurt real bad."

Bile rose in Jenna's throat. "Tell me where you are and I'll come get you."

"I—I tried to . . . go to my sister but . . ."

Jenna's heart hammered loudly inside her chest. "I can't hear you, Rosie. Please tell me where you are."

It seemed to take forever, but Rosalia finally told Jenna her location.

"That's not far from Mavis. I know the hospital there. Stay put, Rosie. I'll call an ambulance for you and meet you at the hospital."

She kept an address book in the drawer of her nightstand. Quickly she flipped to the proper page, dialed the hospital and made the arrangements for Rosalia. She slipped into her robe, then went to find Chase.

He wasn't in the kitchen. She glanced about, noting the breakfast plates stacked in the sink, the half-empty pot of coffee on the stove.

She hurried toward the bathroom. He was probably in there taking a shower.

The bathroom was empty. The towels were folded over the rack in perfect, pristine order.

Her knees grew weak and she held onto the doorjamb for support.

"Chase!" No answer. She could hear the note of fear in her voice. "If you're here, please say something!"

He couldn't have left her there alone, not after last night. Besides, wasn't that part of what the curse was about, seeing to it that they were metaphorically joined at the hip?

He had to be somewhere in the house. She moved from room to room, even the basement, calling his name, praying she could catch the scent of wood smoke and spice in the air, hear his low rumble of laughter, but there was nothing.

He wasn't anywhere except deep inside her heart.

"This isn't funny, Chase," she said as she pulled on a pair of jeans and a sweater. "I hated hide-and-seek as a kid and I don't like it any better now. Rosalia's in trouble. We have to go help her."

She gathered up her purse, car keys and jacket and strode to the front door. "You can't leave without me. I can't leave without you." Wherever he was in the house, this would force the issue. Unless he was unconscious somewhere—God forbid—he'd show up.

He didn't.

Alone, she opened the door and stepped outside. No unseen forces held her captive. No mysterious entity barred her way.

Face it, Jenna, he's gone. It's happened again. You've been left behind.

"No!" She closed the door behind her and forced a deep breath into her lungs. He wouldn't do that, not after last night.

Don't you get it, you fool? The curse is broken. He got what he wanted. He's gone.

Tears pressed hard against the backs of her eyelids, but she refused to let them fall. There was nothing to cry about. She had to believe that...dear God, she wanted to believe that.

She felt as if she were being torn in half by opposing emotions. She wanted to go into the house and search every corner, every nook and cranny, for clues to Chase's disappearance, but there was Rosalia to consider. The young woman had no money. She was terrified and alone, and only the doctors knew how badly Gil had hurt her.

Heart breaking, Jenna climbed into her car and drove toward the hospital.

"He hasn't left me," she told herself as she maneuvered the dark roads. Just because she couldn't see or hear him was no reason to believe he'd walked out on her. What was that he'd told her, that he'd been with her for days before she finally saw him and believed in his existence? Maybe he was sitting next to her right now and she just couldn't see him.

She glanced at the passenger seat, praying for some sign, some hint that he was there with her, but her heart sank. There was one sitting there, same as there was no one in her bed and no one in her house and no one in her life.

Not now.

Not ever.

IT WAS EVEN COLDER than the last time, but maybe that was because now he finally understood warmth.

The first time Chase had been here, he'd had nothing to lose except a career. There had been nothing at stake except the million-dollar contract he was sure would come from his stunt here at the mine.

Now everything was different. Now there was Jenna, beautiful Jenna with the soft heart and luminous soul. Jenna who'd made him feel alive... who'd made him *feel*.

Maybe that was the real curse. To go through eternity knowing he'd come so close to heaven, only to have it split between his fingers.

Knowing that she was out there alone.

The world was a cruel place. He knew that better than most, and he suspected she did, as well. But when he was with her, he could almost believe in happy endings.

Almost.

The darkness pulled him down deeper and deeper.

It wouldn't be long now.

"ARE YOU the next of kin?" the nurse at the desk asked Jenna an hour later.

"Oh, God," Jenna whispered. "No...please, no."

The nurse reached out to steady her. "Ms. Suarez is in the O.R. We need the information for our records."

Jenna sagged against the desk, feeling as if someone had turned her bones to rubber. "How—how badly hurt is she?" she asked as she began to fill out the intricate forms that would see to it that Rosalia's medical bills were covered.

"She is in grave condition, Ms. Grey, but Dr. Watkins is our best thoracic surgeon. We'll keep you informed."

It was hard to think about Rosalia lying in there on the operating table and not want to take Gil apart with her bare hands.

She called both Liz and Grace to tell them what had happened. She left a message on Mavis's answering machine. She paced the length of the waiting room, praying for Rosalia, thinking of Chase, wondering how it was her life had become such a mess.

Last night there had been no barriers between her heart and his. They had talked about their childhoods. She told him things she'd never told another living person. He'd told her about the loneliness at the center of his soul. That meant something, maybe even more than the wild splendor they'd found in each other's arms.

You're good at that, Jenna, remember? You don't break their hearts, you put them back together again.

She stepped outside into the cool night air and looked at the stars. He hadn't made any promises to her last night. None of those romantic declarations she'd read about in books or seen in the movies. And how could he? Their entire relationship had been based on an illusion as fragile as a soap bubble. The illusion of love. Of permanence. That together they were stronger than forces neither understood.

And maybe they had been, if only for a moment. Maybe he had walked out her door and back into the life he'd left behind, and she'd be nothing more than a fond memory.

"Jenna! I was hopin' I'd find you here."

She peered into the darkness. "Mavis! You got my message."

The old woman moved quickly up the pathway until she was at Jenna's side. "How is Rosalia?"

"They don't know yet. She's been in surgery for hours." She quickly detailed Rosa's injuries and the prognosis. "Guarded optimism."

Mavis uttered a string of harsh statements about Gil, all of which Jenna agreed with. "The son of a bitch belongs behind bars," Mavis said. "And you can count on me to testify when the time comes."

Jenna gave her a swift hug. "I love you, Mavis," she said, her voice breaking with emotion.

"Now what are you doing here?" Mavis demanded in a surprising about-face. "Don't you have someplace else to go?"

Jenna wiped her eyes with the back of her hand. "He's gone."

"Damn right he's gone. That's part of the curse."

Jenna felt as if she'd received a jolt of electricity. "What do you mean, that's part of the curse? What do you know about the curse?" Mavis hadn't known anything special about it the other day.

"Where do you think I've been all day, girl, playin' bingo? I did some investigating, same as you should've been doing if you and that boy hadn't been so preoccupied."

"You're scaring me, Mavis. Have you found something out?" *Is there a chance for us? Could there possibly be a chance?*

"He's at the mine."

Her body jerked with shock. "How can you be so sure?"

"I spoke to old lady Willow down at the home past Branchwater. The town clerk told me her grandma's the one who died in the mine, and she says it's a love curse."

"Meaning what?"

"Meaning true love is the only antidote."

A hysterical laugh burst from Jenna's throat. "Why don't you throw in the ruby slippers while you're at it, Mavis? Who can say what true love is or isn't?"

"Do you love him?" Mavis asked.

You've known it from the first moment you saw him, Jenna. He's the other half of your soul. "Oh, Mavis," she whispered, filled with a painful mix of hope and loss. "I love him more than life itself."

"Then go to him, girl. Fight for him if you have to. Just don't let it all slip away like those damn fools did one hundred years ago."

She remembered the story of the three people who had died in the mine. A lonely wife and two weak men, neither of whom loved her enough to save her.

"I don't understand," she said, grabbing Mavis's hands in hers. "How do I know he'll be there?"

"Ain't nothin' for sure in this world, girl. Sometimes you just have to close your eyes and jump right in."

"Rosalia," she said, gesturing toward the waiting room. "I promised I'd be here for her."

"And you will be," Mavis said, "later on. You've been doin' for others as long as I've known you. It's time you did what's right for yourself."

"You'll stay here for Rosie?"

Mavis nodded. "Just as long as she wants me."

She was gone before Mavis finished the sentence.

SHE DROVE FLAT OUT toward the mine, as fast as the VW could manage. To hell with speed limits. Time was running out.

She'd noticed a car following her the first few miles or so but she'd accelerated and apparently left him eating dust.

It was eleven forty-five when she screeched to a stop by the Danger sign. The boards had been removed and lay now on the ground. A wash of moonlight drifted across the craggy opening to the mine, making the whole thing seem surreal, like the surface of the moon. A car's engine rumbled somewhere in the distance, but it barely registered on her. The Tucker Mine was old news. There'd be nobody else stopping here tonight but her.

She turned off the VW's engine and was enveloped by the quiet. Heart thundering inside her chest, she climbed out of the car and approached the entrance to the mine. *Only fools enter here,* went the curse. *What you most fear is what you must face.*

A life without him, she thought as she stepped into the unknown. Facing that was like facing a chain of days and nights of bone-deep loneliness without beginning or end. The way her life had been before she opened her heart and soul to love.

She shivered as she stepped deeper into the mine. It was cold and damp, much colder than she'd realized it would be. The darkness was so complete she couldn't see her hand in front of her face, and she moved slowly, cautiously, fearful both of what she might find . . . and what she might not.

She stumbled once over a rock and fell to one knee. Gravel dug into her flesh, and she knew she was probably bleeding. It didn't matter. The only thing that mattered was finding Chase before it was too late.

Time slowed to a crawl. Seconds seemed like hours. It had to be nearly midnight.

"Please, Chase," she whispered as she inched her way down a sharp and unexpected slope. "Please be here."

Not even fate would be so cruel as to bring them together only to rip them apart.

She heard a rustling sound to her left then caught the faintest scent of wood smoke and spice. She reached out in the darkness but felt nothing. Her disappointment lay bitter against her tongue. She took another step forward, then another, then stumbled again. But this time the barrier was larger, more substantial. More human?

"Chase!" Her voice pierced the silence, ricocheted off the walls. "My God, it's you! I know it's you!"

Silence.

Deep and absolute.

"Say something, Chase! Please." She knelt beside him and placed her head against his chest. He was alive. Thank God in heaven, he was still alive. Instinctively she knew he hadn't met with an accident, that this was part of the curse, the final part, and that she had only a handful of minutes to save him. "I love you!" she cried out. "I can't live without you."

"And ain't that too damn bad." A bright light flared some twenty feet away from her, illuminating a face.

Some people said evil didn't exist, but in that moment Jenna knew they were wrong. Hell existed. She saw it in the eyes of the man standing before her holding a gun on her.

Gil kept the flashlight trained full on her face as he moved toward her. "It's all your fault, bitch." His footsteps sounded closer. "I wouldn't have had to do it if you'd kept your nose out of our business."

"Rosalia's not your business any longer, Gil." She tried not to shield her eyes against the painful glare.

"The hell she's not." He moved closer, still aiming that gun at her head. "Got her in some damn hospital."

"You almost killed her," Jenna snapped. "She's in surgery."

"Your fault," Gil said. "Your damn fault."

Oh, God, she thought. *He's drunk.* If she'd had any chance at all of reasoning with him, it had drowned in a bottle of cheap whiskey and a six-pack.

Behind her Chase stirred. It must be almost midnight. Was this how it was going to end for them? So close to a happy ending that she could reach out and touch it . . . yet so far.

"I gotta do this," Gil said. "I told you not to come between me and my woman and you din't listen to me. You din't listen."

He dropped the flashlight to the ground. A beam of light shot deep into the mine. He gripped the gun with two hands.

"Say good-night, bitch."

CHASE WAS FALLING, falling, faster and faster, end over end, dropping through cold, black space toward nothingness, when it happened.

She needed him.

Strength filled his limbs and his heart. Righteous anger flooded his brain. He reversed direction and started climbing, moving swiftly upward with a fierceness of will unlike anything he'd never known.

He grabbed Jenna by the shoulders and forced her behind an outcropping of rock. Then with a roar he flung himself at the son of a bitch who'd threatened to take her life. The guy ducked, trying to elude him, but he shifted his weight and found his target.

"He can see you!" Jenna screamed. "My God, he can see you!"

Her words didn't register. He tried for the gun but Gil knocked him off balance and he fell against a rock. He launched himself at the guy's midsection and they both tumbled to the ground. He heard Jenna moving behind him, saw the beam from the flashlight shifting, arcing overhead, as she grabbed for it.

"Stop!"

She wouldn't listen. That beautiful, spectacular woman wielded the flashlight like a mighty weapon and started for Gil, using her anger like a shield.

The gun clattered to the ground. The bastard leapt for it. In the blink of an eye Gil had it aimed straight at Jenna, straight at the woman who had given him the one glimpse of happiness he would ever know.

With a cry that came from the depths of his soul, he threw himself in the line of fire and took the bullet that was meant for her.

THE MINE ECHOED with her screams as Chase crumpled to the ground at her feet, a deep red stain spreading across the front of his shirt.

"Not now!" She cradled him against her body as Gil's footsteps faded in the distance. "Don't leave me...please don't leave me." She'd spent her whole life saying goodbye and she didn't want to say goodbye again.

They were part of each other. Their souls were linked. Their hearts beat as one. They couldn't be torn away from each other, not now, not when they had finally found each other.

"I love you," she whispered, her tears falling on his ashen face. "Dear God, how I love you."

His eyes opened and he tried to focus in on her. His lips parted but no sound came out.

I'm losing you, she thought as her heart threatened to break. *And there's nothing I can do to save you.* Her fallen angel. Her love.

"L-listen..." He felt as if he was floating a great distance away from his body, and it took all of his concentration to form the simple word.

She brought her ear to his lips. He caught the familiar scent of her skin, and a sense of peace washed over him. She lived. That was enough for this lifetime.

"Love you..." It was the best he could do. He hoped she knew all that went with it.

Later on there would be time to think about those words, to hold them close, to whisper them in the dark of night when she was alone again and lonely. "Hold on," she begged him even as she saw him fading away in front of her very eyes, even as she knew he was dying. Dear God, she hadn't realized a man could lose so much blood and still live. "I'm not going to lose you!"

Enough. The voice seemed to emanate from somewhere deep inside her chest, as much a sense of light as sound.

"Who are you?" she asked, holding Chase even closer. "What do you want?"

You have both done well. We are satisfied.

"Where are you?"

That is not important.

This is going to sound crazy, Chase had said, but there was this voice . . .

"Help us," she demanded, too heartsick to be afraid. "Save him if you can."

He has found the secret. He can save himself.

"Damn you!" she exploded. "I don't care about secrets. I love him!" Her voice caught. "I love him," she repeated, "and I'm not going to lose him."

The laughter felt strange against her rib cage. *It has already been done.*

"That's impossible! I—" She looked at her hands. The bloodstains were gone. She placed her palms against his shirtfront. The fabric was smooth and untouched. "My God!" Her tears turned to ones of joy.

You will lead him on a merry chase through the years, Jenna Grey, but he is a lucky man.

"Wait!" she cried out. "Who are you? I want to thank you."

Your children and your children's children will grow strong and honorable. That is thanks enough.

She asked no more questions after that. She didn't need to. All the answers she needed were right there in her arms.

She sat very still, holding the man she loved against her breast, and she waited for him to come back to her.

And he would come back to her. The joy that flooded her soul was too splendid to be contained. She needed to share that joy with him, to tell him the things she'd only whispered inside her heart, to plan for a future she suddenly believed was theirs for the taking.

CHASE AWAKENED SLOWLY, as if he was climbing up through a thick fog. *The end of the road,* he thought. Somehow he'd believed they were going to beat the odds, but all hope was gone. Gil's bullet had seen to that. He sucked in a deep breath, expecting to feel the rib-crushing pain in the middle of his chest where the bullet had struck.

He felt nothing.

He sucked in a second deep breath. His lungs filled effortlessly with air.

Was this heaven?

He opened his eyes and saw Jenna looking at him. *My wife,* he thought, savoring the word. But what was she doing there in heaven with him?

"It's over," she whispered, in a voice rich with love and longing. "You're back."

He struggled to make sense of the words. "Heaven," he managed. "Is this—?"

Those beautiful turquoise eyes of hers swam with tears. "Oh, yes," she said. "This most definitely is heaven." At the look on his face she laughed softly. "Heaven on earth."

"I'm not dead?"

She shook her head.

"The curse. Is it—"

"Broken," she said. "It was so simple, Chase. The simplest solution possible."

Suddenly it all made perfect sense. It wasn't marriage he'd been afraid of, it was the power and wonder of love, of handing your heart and soul into the care of another person, of being loved in return.

"I love you, Jenna." There was a lifetime of loneliness in those simple words ... and a lifetime of hope.

"And it's a darn good thing," she said, touching his cheek with a gentle hand, "because I have no intention of letting you go."

He couldn't have said it better himself.

Epilogue

Christmas Day — Two months later

"The turkey doesn't look right." Jenna peered into the oven. "Shouldn't it be browner by now?" Thank God Rosalia and Mavis were bringing the vegetables. Poultry was proving to be more than she could handle.

"Quit worrying," her husband said, grabbing her up in his arms. "It has another few hours."

He felt so strong, so warm. Would she ever get used to the wonder of being loved? "Maybe I should adjust the temperature."

He threw her over his shoulder and started for the bedroom. "Leave the temperature alone. The turkey can take care of itself."

She laughed as they tumbled to the bed. "I should have paid attention at Thanksgiving when Mavis cooked dinner."

"You had other things to worry about at Thanksgiving," he said. "Remember?"

"You're a wicked man!" She tossed a pillow at him. "What if someone had seen us? You're not invisible any longer."

Not even his beloved wife knew just how true that statement was. Every day, in every way, he understood how deeply his life had changed. He was part of the world now, tied into the fabric of everyday life, thoroughly domesticated and loving every minute of it. By opening his heart and soul to Jenna, he had opened himself to the world. And to his amazement the world had welcomed him with open arms.

He was center stage at the Paradise Hotel once again, dazzling people with grand illusions and feats of legerdemain. He loved the applause and adulation, but when you came down to it, none of it mattered a damn without Jenna.

She was the secret to it all. She was every beat of his heart, every breath he drew into his lungs, every dream he would ever dream. All these years of loneliness, of searching for something to give meaning to his life—she'd made it all disappear the moment she looked into his eyes and smiled.

Thanks to Jenna, he finally understood what real magic was all about.

He leaned on his right elbow. "I have something for you."

She waggled her eyebrows mischievously. "That's what I was hoping you'd say." She patted the bed next to her.

He tried to grin, but an onset of nerves tightened his jaw.

"Chase?" She touched his forearm. "Are you okay?"

He nodded, feeling a damn fool lump settle in the middle of his throat. He reached under his pillow and withdrew a small black box. "For you." He handed it to her, wondering if she realized he was handing her his heart.

She studied him, openly curious. "I've never seen you quite like this before," she said, holding the box in her hand. "You're making me nervous."

"Just open it," he said gruffly.

"I'll bet it's those pearl earrings we saw at the mall. You already gave me that beautiful choker for Christmas. They were awfully expensive, Chase, maybe you—" She stopped. She stared. She started to cry. Nestled in the black velvet was a wide golden band, the kind of ring that made you think of forever. The kind of ring you passed on from mother to daughter, from generation to generation. The gold might grow thin with time, but the love, the connection, would only grow stronger.

He took her hand and kissed each fingertip. "I'm asking you to marry me."

Laughter mingled with her tears. "We're already married. We're so married we could be in the *Guinness Book of World Records*." Three ceremonies in less than twenty-four hours certainly qualified for some kind of an award.

"I want the whole deal," he said, fixing her with his golden gaze. "I want the flowers and the music. I want Mavis standing up there in all her finery and Rosalia standing beside you. I want the whole damn world to know we belong to each other, that we're a family. Let's do it, Jenna. We got married those other times for all the wrong reasons. Let's do it this time for the right one, because we love each other and we want the whole damn world to know it."

"There's one other reason for getting married again," she said softly. "A very tiny reason but an important one."

Her words resonated inside his heart.

He saw beyond the bed and the room and the house in the middle of the desert. He saw children. Happy, healthy, surrounded by love. He saw a big house with a swing set in the backyard and a floppy-eared mutt sleeping on the front porch. He saw commotion and he heard laughter and at the center of it all he saw himself and Jenna, fighting and loving and growing old together, the way it was meant to be.

He saw a family. *Their* family.

A family as lasting as the ring of gold she held in her hand, as strong as the forces that had brought them together.

"A baby," he said, placing his palm against her flat stomach.

"Our baby," she whispered, covering his hand with her own.

And then Chase Quinn and Jenna Grey threw back their heads and laughed for joy.

COMING NEXT MONTH

#557 ONCE UPON A HONEYMOON by Julie Kistler

Self-proclaimed bachelor Tripp Ashby was in a no-win situation...and only Bridget Emerick could help him. His old pal had bailed him out since college—but this time, the sexy bachelor needed the unthinkable...a wife! *Don't miss the second book in the STUDS miniseries!*

#558 QUINN'S WAY by Rebecca Flanders
Heartbeat

When David Quinn appeared out of nowhere and entered Houston Malloy's ordered life—mouthwatering smile, bedroom eyes and all—she thought the man was out of this world. Little did she know how right she was!

#559 SECRET AGENT DAD by Leandra Logan

As a secret agent, Michael Hawkes had stared down danger with nerves of steel. But then he found himself protecting his old flame Valerie Warner—and her twins—in the jungles of suburbia. Twins who looked an awful lot like him.... Michael never saw danger like he did now!

#560 FROM DRIFTER TO DADDY by Mollie Molay
Rising Star

For a couple of hundred bucks Sara Martin bought the wrongfully imprisoned drifter Quinn Tucker for thirty days. But it didn't take long for Quinn to know he was safer in jail, doing his time, than he was out on a ranch with a gorgeous woman and her ready-made family....

AVAILABLE THIS MONTH:

HARLEQUIN

AMERICAN ◆ ROMANCE®

Four sexy hunks who vowed they'd never take
"the vow" of marriage...

What happens to this Bachelor Club
when, one by one, they find the right
bachelorette?

Meet four of the most perfect men:

Steve: **THE MARRYING TYPE**
Judith Arnold
(October)

Tripp: **ONCE UPON A HONEYMOON**
Julie Kistler
(November)

Ukiah: **HE'S A REBEL**
Linda Randall Wisdom
(December)

Deke: **THE WORLD'S LAST BACHELOR**
Pamela Browning
(January)

Meet five of the most mysterious, magical men in

These men are more than tall, dark and handsome. They have extraordinary powers that make them "more than men." But whether they are able to grant you three wishes, communicate with dolphins or live forever, make no mistake—their greatest, most extraordinary power is of seduction.

Make a date with all these MORE THAN MEN:

#501	A WISH...AND A KISS by Margaret St. George	$3.50	☐
#517	FOREVER ALWAYS by Rebecca Flanders	$3.50	☐
#525	CINDERMAN by Anne Stuart	$3.50	☐
#538	KISSED BY THE SEA by Rebecca Flanders	$3.50 U.S.	☐
		$3.99 CAN.	☐

(limited quantities available on certain titles)

TOTAL AMOUNT	$
POSTAGE & HANDLING	$
($1.00 for one book, 50¢ for each additional)	
APPLICABLE TAXES*	$
TOTAL PAYABLE	$
(check or money order—please do not send cash)	

To order, complete this form and send it, along with a check or money order for the total above, payable to Harlequin Books, to: **In the U.S.:** 3010 Walden Avenue, P.O. Box 9047, Buffalo, NY 14269-9047; **In Canada:** P.O. Box 613, Fort Erie, Ontario, L2A 5X3.

Name: _____

Address: _____ City: _____

State/Prov.: _____ Zip/Postal Code: _____

*New York residents remit applicable sales taxes.
 Canadian residents remit applicable GST and provincial taxes.

MTMORDER1

"HOORAY FOR HOLLYWOOD" SWEEPSTAKES

HERE'S HOW THE SWEEPSTAKES WORKS

OFFICIAL RULES — NO PURCHASE NECESSARY

To enter, complete an Official Entry Form or hand print on a 3" x 5" card the words "HOORAY FOR HOLLYWOOD", your name and address and mail your entry in the pre-addressed envelope (if provided) or to: "Hooray for Hollywood" Sweepstakes, P.O. Box 9076, Buffalo, NY 14269-9076 or "Hooray for Hollywood" Sweepstakes, P.O. Box 637, Fort Erie, Ontario L2A 5X3. Entries must be sent via First Class Mail and be received no later than 12/31/94. No liability is assumed for lost, late or misdirected mail.

Winners will be selected in random drawings to be conducted no later than January 31, 1995 from all eligible entries received.

Grand Prize: A 7-day/6-night trip for 2 to Los Angeles, CA including round trip air transportation from commercial airport nearest winner's residence, accommodations at the Regent Beverly Wilshire Hotel, free rental car, and $1,000 spending money. (Approximate prize value which will vary dependent upon winner's residence: $5,400.00 U.S.); 500 Second Prizes: A pair of "Hollywood Star" sunglasses (prize value: $9.95 U.S. each). Winner selection is under the supervision of D.L. Blair, Inc., an independent judging organization, whose decisions are final. Grand Prize travelers must sign and return a release of liability prior to traveling. Trip must be taken by 2/1/96 and is subject to airline schedules and accommodations availability.

Sweepstakes offer is open to residents of the U.S. (except Puerto Rico) and Canada who are 18 years of age or older, except employees and immediate family members of Harlequin Enterprises, Ltd., its affiliates, subsidiaries, and all agencies, entities or persons connected with the use, marketing or conduct of this sweepstakes. All federal, state, provincial, municipal and local laws apply. Offer void wherever prohibited by law. Taxes and/or duties are the sole responsibility of the winners. Any litigation within the province of Quebec respecting the conduct and awarding of prizes may be submitted to the Regie des loteries et courses du Quebec. All prizes will be awarded; winners will be notified by mail. No substitution of prizes are permitted. Odds of winning are dependent upon the number of eligible entries received.

Potential grand prize winner must sign and return an Affidavit of Eligibility within 30 days of notification. In the event of non-compliance within this time period, prize may be awarded to an alternate winner. Prize notification returned as undeliverable may result in the awarding of prize to an alternate winner. By acceptance of their prize, winners consent to use of their names, photographs, or likenesses for purpose of advertising, trade and promotion on behalf of Harlequin Enterprises, Ltd., without further compensation unless prohibited by law. A Canadian winner must correctly answer an arithmetical skill-testing question in order to be awarded the prize.

For a list of winners (available after 2/28/95), send a separate stamped, self-addressed envelope to: Hooray for Hollywood Sweepstakes 3252 Winners, P.O. Box 4200, Blair, NE 68009.

CBSRLS

OFFICIAL ENTRY COUPON

"Hooray for Hollywood"
SWEEPSTAKES!

Yes, I'd love to win the Grand Prize — a vacation in Hollywood — or one of 500 pairs of "sunglasses of the stars"! Please enter me in the sweepstakes!

This entry must be received by December 31, 1994.
Winners will be notified by January 31, 1995.

Name _____

Address _____ Apt. _____

City _____

State/Prov. _____ Zip/Postal Code _____

Daytime phone number _____
(area code)

Account # _____

Return entries with invoice in envelope provided. Each book in this shipment has two entry coupons — and the more coupons you enter, the better your chances of winning!

DIRCBS

OFFICIAL ENTRY COUPON

"Hooray for Hollywood"
SWEEPSTAKES!

Yes, I'd love to win the Grand Prize — a vacation in Hollywood — or one of 500 pairs of "sunglasses of the stars"! Please enter me in the sweepstakes!

This entry must be received by December 31, 1994.
Winners will be notified by January 31, 1995.

Name _____

Address _____ Apt. _____

City _____

State/Prov. _____ Zip/Postal Code _____

Daytime phone number _____
(area code)

Account # _____

Return entries with invoice in envelope provided. Each book in this shipment has two entry coupons — and the more coupons you enter, the better your chances of winning!

DIRCBS